LETTING IN THE NIGHT

Also by Joan Lindau

Mrs. Cooper's Boardinghouse

LETTING IN THE NIGHT

a novel by

JOAN LINDAU

Firebrand
Books
Ithaca, New York

Book design by Betsy Bayley
Cover art and design by Catherine Hopkins
Typesetting by Bets Ltd.

Printed in the United States on acid-free paper by McNaughton &
Gunn.

Library of Congress Cataloging-in-Publication Data

Lindau, Joan.
    Letting in the light.

    I. Title.
PS3562.I496L4   1989   813'.54   89–1331
ISBN 0–932379–60–5 (alk. paper)
ISBN 0–932379–59–1 (pbk. : alk. paper)

to Catherine, with all my love

Saturday, December 14
San Francisco

I feel sad today and I can't explain it because nothing sad has happened to me lately. Feeling low on a grey, rainy day wouldn't surprise me, but today is brilliant. I sit on my steps and wait for the mail to arrive and try not to think about the Christmas cards I haven't begun to write.

Every year I've lived here, where it is still green and flowering in December, I've been caught off guard by Christmas. Perhaps that is it. I grew up in Michigan where there was usually snow on the ground by now. I miss that, I suppose.

A letter from Franco arrives in my mail, and with her letter an invitation to spend Christmas with her. It is so nearly a wish come true. But her letter says she is sick.

> Dear Thad,
>
> Last month I was in New York Hospital, my old stomping grounds, to have some tests. For some time now, I haven't been able to pull myself out of a peculiar tiredness.
>
> I half expected I'd be told I was imagining it and I had my defenses up for that. I wasn't at all prepared for what it turns out to be: Lou Gehrig's disease, Amyotrophic Lateral Sclerosis.

I've been wrestling with this for weeks. Surprisingly enough, knowing your life's just been shortened by thirty years has its up side. It does take the pressure off having to do and face certain things.

I didn't think I'd want to see anyone this Christmas, but two days ago I woke from a nap wishing you were here. It would be good to have someone other than myself and my situation to focus on. I don't want to spend Christmas alone or with anyone else. Please come and spend it with me. I think I'll be good enough company.

You should probably give yourself a day or two for this to sink in and then decide if it would be good for you to come. I'm prepared for the disappointment that at this late date it might be next to impossible, if not impossible, to get here.

There's no change in me except the physical one. I don't know why I'm not turned upside down and inside out, but I'm not.

It's been snowing, hard at times, for two days, so it looks like we'll have a white Christmas.

Love,
Franco

I get up and instead of going into the house, I step down to the sidewalk and start down the street. I'm several blocks before I'm aware that I'm crying and that Edna is with me. She looks up at me with her ears perked and her light brown eyes searching for what is wrong with me. I bend down to reassure her, then continue walking to the end of the block.

On the steps at Baker and Broadway I can see the San Francisco Bay. There are only a few boats out on the water, not like two months ago, but it is as warm and beautiful a day for sailing as October was. This contrast to the cold climate Franco is experiencing underlines the distance between us and makes me feel out of place here. But my longing now isn't for snow or for place.

I glance down at Franco's letter, written on Woodbine stationery. She was always the strongest, most athletic, and most spirited of friends. It is hard to imagine her tired, let alone sick. I try to recall a time when Franco was sick, and all I can remember is a summer when she got sunburned so badly she couldn't put clothes on for two days. Is it possible that during the three years we lived together at Woodbine and the three years following, when we saw one another every weekend, she was never ill? Could such a vigorous immune system suddenly fail? How is it she is not turned inside out? I read her letter again, searching for clues to the down side she does not mention.

Would I go? There was no question about it. Franco was polite and suggested a way out for me, but she, too, knows I'll be there.

I was walking back to my dorm from the library, one January afternoon, when I saw a handful of students sledding on the slope behind Ellenby Hall. The first men to be enrolled and graduate from Woodbine College were in Franco's and my class. There were only a handful of them. Before that, Woodbine had been a women's college. I stopped to watch these oddballs, expecting the one wearing knickers and a peacoat to land in the pond at the bottom of the slope. Instead, he veers toward me.

"Want to have a go?" he asks.

I don't answer right away because I'm startled by his feminine voice.

"Come on," Franco says. "I can tell you'd like to. We'll go together," she insists. And so we did.

The mixed group of us walked over to Duffy's when it got dark. There wasn't enough room for all of us at a single booth, so Franco and I sit at a separate one.

"My name is Frances Cole," she says, smiling across at me, "but everyone calls me Franco." She unbuttons her coat and pulls off her stocking cap. Thick, blonde hair bounces free, and she runs her fingers through it several times.

The liveliness of Franco's smile and hair excite me, and her blue eyes, which won't let go of mine, make me self-conscious. I feel for the first time what I had been expected to feel but did not feel toward the boys in high school.

Franco lived in a rooming house on Willis Street. She shared quarters with a girl who would leave school to marry a boy at Cornell. When this happened, Franco invited me to take her roommate's place, and Franco and I lived together on Willis Street for the next three years. I can still recall the smell of the paint baking on the radiator in our room, and I will always associate it with romance.

I get up from the stone step where I've been sitting and rub my cold fanny until the feeling returns to it. Then Edna and I start home. We pass the El Drisco Hotel, a neighborhood polling place where I help out on election days. The desk clerk, in conversation with someone under the canopy, notices us and waves.

Franco and I had breakfast at the El Drisco seven years ago when she was out here to give a paper at Stanford. She wasn't herself on that visit. She seemed lethargic, even melancholy, and when I asked her she said her work was getting her down. But perhaps Franco was already sick and didn't realize it. Disease is the last thing anyone willful ever suspects.

Back at the house, I go to my desk to look over the other mail that came. It's pointless, I realize, and I give it up to call the airlines.

Martha tries to reach me while I'm on the phone getting reservations, and when she finally does, she asks me who the hell I've been talking to for so long. I don't tell her. I can't bring myself to speak the truth.

"Do you want me to come over there?" she asks.

"Why?" I say, acting surprised.

"You don't sound like yourself. Are you all right?"

"I'm fine," I say, and she doesn't insist.

I hang up the phone, and the quiet which follows is unsettling. I go to the bathroom and turn the tub water on full force. All those muscles I've been straining in order to keep a hold of myself relax in the bath. Edna hears me and comes trotting in. I stick my arm out of the tub to quiet her whimpering.

———

The Christmas following our graduation from Woodbine, Franco invited me to go home with her to Newark, New Jersey, where she'd grown up. She was in Baltimore at Johns Hopkins at the time; I was at Columbia and had no family to spend the holiday with. My brother was thirteen and I was eleven when our parents died; the grandmother who raised us had died within the past year; and Wesley was stationed in Vietnam.

Franco warned me it would be crowded and that we would have to share a bathroom with her three sisters and brother. I couldn't wait. In college Franco had complained to me about the noise and confusion and lack of privacy in her home, and I had listened with envy. She would groan about going home for visits while I longed in silence for her to invite me to go with her, and when she returned to school I would overwhelm her with questions about her family. She had a richness she took so for granted that she thought I was only being polite when I asked about her sisters and brother.

One time she did say to me, "Relax, Thad, you don't have to be polite with me."

"I'm not!" I answered, and she gave me that look of hers—that I-know-better-than-anyone look—which Franco was famous for giving her friends.

Franco believed she knew best about nearly everything, and she did often enough to get away with that arrogance. She was not only the top student in our class, but possibly the most liked. She put forth a great deal of effort toward academic success, and none toward the other.

———

After taking a bath, I make myself a sandwich, watch the news, and go to bed. I don't have trouble falling asleep, but I wake in the middle of the night feeling something bad has happened and not clear what.

Sunday, December 15
San Francisco

Nothing goes right this morning. Stripping the bed, I bang my shinbone hard on the side of the bed. Then, in the bathroom, I drop the water glass in the sink and cut my finger badly. I give Edna some new dog food that has pieces in it, and she takes it out of her bowl, bit by bit, and spits it on the floor around her bowl before going back to eat it. Sometimes she disgusts me.

Finally, I go to get a box of old journals down from the top shelf of my closet, and because my finger is so damn sore, I drop the box and everything falls out of it onto the floor. It is more than I can handle. I sit down on the floor and have another good cry.

Edna comes running in to me. I'm still disgusted with her, so I push her away, and she goes just outside the bedroom door to lie down in the hall with her chin on the floor and her sad eyes looking back at me.

"Get out of here!" I yell at her, and she runs away.

I sweep my arm across the floor, scattering my journals, then cry some more. My grandmother tried to tone me down by telling me I had a dangerous temper, but I held onto it, feeling my brother's acquiescence was cowardice.

After a few moments to calm down, I pick up one of my journals and look through it.

January 10, 1967: . . . Franco's the star in her family. They all gather around her and fire questions at her and eat up everything she tells them. And she's so sincere about answering their questions she doesn't even realize the dynamic of the thing. Now that's concentration!

Mrs. Cole poked her head into the living room when all this was going on to say it was time to take the door down, and Franco interrupted herself to say, ''I thought we were going to eat from our laps.''

''A table will be easier,'' her mother said.

The kitchen door came down off its hinges and was placed on sawhorses to serve as a dining table. Franco was horrified.

I told Franco later that I admired her mother's resourcefulness, and Franco gave me a look. You can't tell that Franco anything.

I pick my journals up off the floor, return them to the box, and get dressed. Then Edna and I go out for a walk.

Now that we've returned I don't know what to do. I wish I could pack my bags and leave for Woodbine tonight. I've thought about calling Franco, but I'd rather be with her when we talk about what's happened.

Monday, December 16
San Francisco

I put Edna in the backyard this morning because I'm not up to walking over to the park, and she gets out through the back gate when the garbageman comes. I hear the gate open and not close, but it doesn't register in time. I scour the neighborhood and don't find Edna, hiding under a neighbor's porch with a horrible bone, until my third trip around the block. So much for trying to make things easier for myself.

I have breakfast with the "Today Show," but I don't really watch it. I'm back in the kitchen on Willis Street.

———

Franco and I both had an early class our second winter. No one in her right mind signed up for an eight o'clock winter semester; you were transferred into one when the later classes were filled.

I would have stayed in bed longer those cold mornings, and skipped breakfast, if Franco hadn't gotten up and fixed us something to eat. Half asleep, I'd sit at the table and stare off while she dashed around the kitchen.

"What did Alice say about Rainey?" she'd ask in a cheerful

voice which seemed inappropriate for that hour of day. Then,
"Wake up! Thad! What did Alice say?"
"She said she'd been drinking."
"Is she all right?"
"Yes, but the car's not. She totaled it."
"Alice has no sense."
"Alice wasn't drinking," I say, starting to come around.
"If it was my car I wouldn't let anyone drive it, and especially not irresponsible Rainey."
"Not even me?"
"Not anyone."

I agreed with Franco about Rainey, but I always felt Franco's hard-and-fast rules were extreme.

Before leaving the house, I gather up the books due back at the school library and take a box of Christmas cards to write while I'm sitting around today. On my way over to Lone Mountain, I decide to eliminate one of my exam questions from the Women's Lit. group and offer to pay a graduate student to grade the freshman papers for me. Janice would probably be eager to because she has a mild crush on me.

I stare out the window of the classroom while my students write, Christmas cards ignored. When I was a student, I always sat toward the front of my classes next to the windows—close enough to be a part of it all, with an escape to the outside world if I wanted it. I rarely looked out the window in my English classes, but I could describe in detail the lawns, trees, and changing sky outside Pearson and Bradley Halls where I took the required science and math classes.

There was one other windowscape I remember well. It was outside Drake Infirmary where I spent one week my freshman year.

My fourth gloomy day in Drake, Franco arrived, but she had

to stand in the doorway to talk to me because I was contagious. Dressed in baggy ski pants and a pink sweater which is a beautiful color on her, she explained how she tracked me down. The day we met I didn't say which dorm I lived in.

"I work in the bursar's office," she says, fiddling with something in her pocket.

"So you looked up my file. What else did you learn about me?"

"That you're rich as Croesus," she says, laughing.

I want to tell her she has a great laugh but I'm sure that would embarrass us both. "I didn't think that sort of thing was in someone's file," I say instead.

"It is when your grandmother endows the college."

I shrug my shoulders, not wanting to make a big thing out of that.

"I called your room when I found out what dorm you were in, but your roommate wouldn't tell me where you were. I called the next day, and the next, and finally I went over and insisted she tell me where you were. She's very possessive."

"I didn't realize."

"Then you and she aren't close?"

I wasn't positive what Franco meant by close, but the answer was no in any case. Franco looked relieved.

Days later, when I got out of the infirmary, I went by Franco's rooming house to thank her for coming by to see me. She jumped up from her desk when her roommate announced me, giving herself away and making me feel wonderful.

It hurts to recall that bright, energetic Franco, laughing and jumping up out of a chair. I get up and walk over to the window to hide my sadness from the class. A woman crosses McAllister Street, heading for the park with her tennis racket.

She sticks in my mind, and when John asks if I am free for lunch, I say no, pick up a sandwich at a corner place, and drive into the park. I park by the boathouse at Stow Lake and stay in the car to eat my sandwich because I don't want to see anyone or be seen. I think about having to return this evening to go to my ceramics class, knowing if I don't I'll have to explain myself to Martha.

Back on campus, I pick up papers that are drifting in two and three at a time from freshmen I gave a take-home exam to, write a note to Janice and leave it in the graduate box, then walk over to the library before going home.

Not much on ALS. There is much more written about multiple sclerosis. But enough on ALS to dash my hopes that Franco might get over this disease. ". . . progressive muscle weakness and wasting . . . no treatment . . . no cure . . . most patients can expect to live three to five years." What about those that aren't like most? Is it better or worse for them?

I feel jittery inside, and the words become a blur. I look up from the page at the young man sitting quietly across the library table from me. What is he reading, I wonder. Has *he* come here concerned about a child, a friend, a lover, hoping to find something to pin *his* hopes on? No, I don't think so, he doesn't look upset. He's here on an assignment. That's all. I push away from the table and stand, then hurry away.

It was a warm and humid night. For relief I went to the library, the only cool place on campus. As I approach the stacks where I often go to study, I see Franco sitting at the small desk I sit at. I hadn't seen her since my visit to her rooming house months before.

"Hello," I say, and she looks up.

"You startled me," she says, but she doesn't look startled. She stands, and instinctively I start to back away.

"Where are you going?" Franco asks.

I stop in my tracks. "Nowhere," I answer.

"Then come back," she says, and she takes the books I'm carrying from me and sets them down on the desk. I had been holding them so close to my chest that my blouse is damp and wrinkled. Franco doesn't try to hide the fact that she notices this. Instead she reaches her hand up and touches my arm. "You're very warm," she says. Keeping her hand on my arm, she asks, "So you come here often?"

"Almost every night," I answer.

"Alone?" she asks. "No study dates?"

"There aren't too many boys around here, in case you haven't noticed."

"Are there any at home?" Franco asks, and her hand slowly retracts.

"No," I answer. "What about you?"

Franco shakes her head and smiles. "You have the most beautiful face I've ever seen," she says.

I don't know what to say to that.

"I'm starved," Franco says. "Will you go with me to Duffy's?"

I was certain if I took a step my legs would buckle under me.

"Please," she says, and she smiles again.

I would have crawled after that smile if necessary.

I set my books down on the return desk in the literature section, and as I start away the woman behind the desk asks, "Nothing today, Professor Owens?"

"No," I answer. "I'm going away for Christmas."

"Lucky you," she says, and I return her smile.

On my way home from Lone Mountain, I stop by the travel agency and pick up my tickets. As soon as I get home, Edna and I leave to go to the park. I chat briefly with the elegant woman who brings her Russian wolfhound to Alta Plaza. It's a strange sight to see a dachshund chase after a wolfhound. Edna has more nerve than sense and only gets away with it because her friend is gentle and the elegant woman suffers fools gladly.

I turn on "MacNeil-Lehrer" back at home and watch the news while I eat my supper. I try not to think about all those exam papers to be graded, about Christmas, about Franco. Thank

God for television.

After the news I change into my corduroys and sweatshirt and drive over to the deYoung Museum. I get there early enough to speak to Martha before she begins the class. I tell her I got some bad news from Franco and ask if she is free anytime tomorrow. "How bad?" she asks me, and when I seem reluctant to say, she says she is free as soon as she empties the kiln in the morning.

I put glaze on my big bowl with the sprayer tonight. First time I've done that, and the sound of the compressor makes me nervous.

I get home in time to see the last ten minutes of "Monday Night Football." Disappointment: the Rams beat the '49ers. Edna's up on the bed with me, cuddling.

I am worried that I'll be sorry I asked Martha to come by tomorrow. I've spoken of Franco to her, but I've never discussed my deep feelings. I suppose now I will have to.

Tuesday, December 17
San Francisco

I send Franco a telegram first thing this morning. I WILL BE THERE. ARRIVE 8PM THURSDAY. MUST RETURN ON THE 27TH. NO OTHER FLIGHTS OUT. I HATE THAT YOU ARE SICK. AND LOVE THE THOUGHT OF SNOW.

I tried several times to write a letter and gave up because I couldn't say everything I felt and didn't want to say less. Better to be brief and send a telegram. A letter, at this point, wouldn't arrive in time anyway.

After hanging up the phone, I let Edna out to sniff around the backyard while I take a shower. Standing under the spray of water, I mentally cross things off a list I know I won't be able to get done. Don't bother with the cleaners; wear what you've got. Forget about Christmas cards; people will understand. Cancel Friday's dentist appointment and Saturday's hair appointment. And beg off tonight's Christmas party in order to grade papers.

When I get out of the shower I'm surprised to discover it's raining outside. I go to the back door, with just a towel wrapped around me, to let Edna in. Then, instead of coming in out of the rain myself, I stand there in the sudden downpour, crying.

I have to get control over myself, I think. I cannot arrive at Franco's in this state.

Martha appears just after noon. I have soup on and sandwiches made. She brings a bowl I made in class with her, fresh from the kiln. It has a crack in its bottom, but Martha thinks I should go ahead and glaze it. I want to toss it. "Put it away then," she says, "and don't look at it for a couple weeks." I put it in a cupboard to appease her, and we sit down to lunch.

Afterward I give Martha Franco's letter. She reads it, folds it, and hands it back to me.

"This sounds very bad," she says, and I nod my head. "I'm sorry, Thad."

I nod my head again. It's set now, irrevocable. I can't pretend it isn't true, now that I've shared it with someone.

Martha asks me questions I've asked myself. Isn't there anything to be done? How much time has she got? Is it a bad way to die? Was Lou Gehrig a baseball player or a football player?

"Baseball," I answer.

Martha's next question catches me off guard. "Were you and Franco ever intimate?"

I answer stupidly, "What do you mean?" And Martha looks at me the way anyone would look at a dope. "In school," I say, and let it go at that.

We are quiet for a minute or two. I don't try to imagine what Martha is thinking. I'm remembering my first night with Franco and how it was for a long time after that night and how it is now.

"You're still in love with her, aren't you?" Martha asks.

"Yes, I suppose I am."

"This must be hell for you."

"How did you know?" I ask.

"The temperature in the room changes when you talk about her," Martha says, smiling. I am able to smile back. "There haven't been any men, have there?"

"Not as I think you mean it," I say.

In our two years of friendship, Martha and I have never talked about our sexuality. We haven't been secretive with one another; we just haven't talked about our very personal lives.

"You're going, of course."

I nod my head and try hard to hold my tears back.

Martha offers to drive me to the airport on Thursday and look after Edna while I'm away. "I'll miss you," she says, and I look away, desperate to stay calm and not to cry. "What are you most afraid of?" she asks me.

"Of losing her," I answer, and I get up to get myself some Kleenex. "And of how I will be," I say, coming back to the kitchen with a tissue. "I don't want to be like this."

"Wouldn't that be all right?"

"No. Franco won't like me this way."

"Why?"

"She wants me there to distract her."

"I wouldn't be so sure. It would be easier to believe that she wants you there because you matter most to her."

I step over to the window where the rain against the pane makes everything beyond a blur. "Either way, this is going to be excruciating. If Christmas is wonderful, I will ache when it's over. And if it's not, if it's a disappointment, I will ache all the while."

"Yes, it's going to be hard."

I'm grateful Martha doesn't give me a pep talk.

Before she leaves I put a load of laundry in and show her how the washer operates in case she wants to use it. She teases me about giving her laundry instructions, and I admit it is only a ploy to keep her with me a while longer. She offers to stay with me all day, but I convince her I have plenty to keep me busy and my mind on track. When she leaves I feel sad, but I am glad she came by.

I would like to believe what Martha said, that Franco wants me with her because I matter most to her, but I have never felt confident of that.

During our graduate years I went down to Baltimore two weekends a month to see Franco, and she, in turn, came up to New York twice a month to see me. It was better for me when I went down to Baltimore because when Franco came up to New York, she always stopped in to see Peter at New York Hospital.

I was jealous of Peter from the start. He and Franco were in nearly every class together at Woodbine. They shared an ambition to be research scientists. They talked for hours about things I was ignorant of. I felt like an outsider when he was present. And afterward, if I complained or appeared hurt, Franco would defend herself and Peter. I couldn't win; it was always two against one.

Christmas, our third year in graduate school, Franco and I took a train to Montreal, and our first night at the inn where we were staying, Franco announced that she was coming to New York to join Peter's lab. She expected me to be thrilled by this decision—no more seeing one another weekends only; we could live together again. But darkness closed in all around me. I felt threatened by Peter. We dressed for dinner in silence.

In the dining room I say to Franco, "Why do you want to work with him? He'll try to lord it over you. You don't need him. You're smarter than he is."

Franco does not answer me. If necessary, she will pretend I'm not even there.

Instead of giving up, I continue, my criticism of Peter becoming more and more personal and exaggerated. Until, finally, Franco is forced to defend Peter, and I feel justified in suspecting her loyalty to him is greater than her loyalty to me. I am satisfactorily hurt.

Franco gets up from the table, and I eat alone.

"I need to ask you just one thing," I say to Franco when I join her in our room upstairs. "Then, I promise, I will drop it."

"What is it?" she asks.

"Are you coming to New York to be with me or Peter?"

"I'm not coming to New York to be with Peter. I'm coming to work with him."

"What about me? Am I just a convenience?"

"What do you want, Thad?"

I couldn't say I want to know how important I am to you, or I want to know how much you love me. I was terrified that her answer would be unacceptable.

Weakly, I asked instead, "Isn't there anyone else to work with?"

"It's a good lab, Thad. Don't you care about that?"

I say yes. She probably knows better.

"Then celebrate with me," she says.

I should have. I might have saved the day and much more. Franco was looking at me at that moment with interest. I turned away to reject her as I felt she had rejected me, and her expression changed from inclination to indifference.

She took a pillow off the bed and a blanket, and she gave them to me. "Find yourself some other place to sleep," she said, and she got into the bed.

I returned to New York, telling myself that in spite of this spat she would come to New York and we would live together. Maybe I let myself think that so I could feel truly wronged when it turned out Franco made other plans—to live alone in an apartment house across the street from New York Hospital.

I applied to Stanford's Ph.D. program and went up to Woodbine to speak with Nell. Helen Glass was Chair of the English Department at Woodbine. She had gone to Stanford.

We had a long talk. She was the first person I spoke to openly about being a lesbian. She didn't advise me to stay at Columbia and she didn't encourage me to leave. She listened to everything I said and was not embarrassed by my confession. Then she gave me a letter of recommendation and suggested I follow my conscience.

I followed it to California.

Wednesday, December 18
San Francisco

I set a bluebook down on the stack on my bedside table and glance at the clock. I could read another, but I ought to get a good night's sleep. I shouldn't even write in my journal. If I lived with someone I might not do this every night; I might talk instead to put the day's events in perspective.

I began writing notes to myself when I was very young. I couldn't tell my friends that my mother and father drank until they got drunk, night after night and often during the days. I couldn't tell anyone what they said and did when they drank. But I found if I wrote down the truth and how I felt about it, I would feel better afterward. I don't have any of those early journals. When my mother and father died I destroyed them.

Today begins earlier than usual so I can clean the house before leaving for the college. It's hard enough to return home after being away, let alone return to a dirty house.

Two students are waiting for me in my office when I get there, to ask if they can take incompletes. I don't have the time or the inclination to listen to their reasons; without debate I say O.K. and leave them standing with their mouths hanging open. I hurry on to Bruce Hall to give the Women in Literature group their exam.

They have such a lust to know what their great-grandmothers read and wrote and how they felt about their lives—their frustrations, their achievements, their secret desires—that in truth, they don't need me.

When I return to the office, all has changed. A wreath is on the door, a tree is up with lights blinking, and carols are playing over the intercom system.

Janice is waiting for me, and I give her the freshman books. She asks me what I'm doing for Christmas. I say I'll be spending it with a very close friend, wanting to leave the impression with her that I am attached to someone. Janice is young enough to be my daughter, but very little seems inappropriate to twenty-one-year-olds.

I have meetings all afternoon and don't leave the office until six. I go down to Orvis's to get Franco a bird feeder and am home by seven to take Edna over to the park. We walk home in the dark, passing house after house decorated with Christmas lights.

This will be the longest Edna and I have been separated. I left her with her mother for a couple of days five years ago. She was only months old then, and the breeder where I'd gotten her obliged me. I went to visit Franco and propose I move back East to live and work with her. Franco had left Peter's side at the lab and was teaching at Woodbine. I thought she would welcome my proposal. I was wrong.

"You're not serious?" she says, when I tell her why I'm there.

"Do you think I came all this way just to kid around?"

"But you're tenured."

"So what? I don't need the security."

"What would you do here?"

"Same thing I do out there. Teach English. I'm sure Nell would—"

"It's a bad idea, Thad."

"The idea isn't bad, Franco. Why can't you just say you don't want me."

"It's not that."

"The hell it isn't."

"You see how easily your feelings get hurt. That's why I can't say things."

"Say it, Franco. And, please, don't spare my feelings."

"I've never lived with anyone."

"For god's sake, Franco, you lived with me."

"When we were eighteen. We're twice that now. It's not like it was then. We're—"

"Oh, shut up. I don't need to hear any more. You're right, it was a lousy idea."

Franco looked terribly guilty. It didn't make sense then, or later upon reflection. It was not like Franco to feel guilty about doing what was best for her. I suspected she was involved with someone. I didn't ask.

At home, I set up the ironing board, and Edna curls up on her pillow under the kitchen table. I watch "River Journeys" on television while I iron what I'll be wearing tomorrow.

I still have the luggage I went away to college with. It's that heavy, leather stuff. I don't use it for travel any more; I use it to store things. The suitcase is dusty from being ignored in the back of my closet. I wipe it off and empty its contents into a dresser drawer I keep for guests, then pack my clothes for Christmas in the suitcase.

As I set off for Woodbine College twenty-four years ago, I worried that people in New York state might be different from the folks in Michigan, that I might not fit in. Nonetheless, I was thrilled about leaving home for the first time. Some people are reluctant to give up childhood; I was in a hurry and assumed all you had to do to be a grownup was leave home. I landed that autumn day at Albany airport, rented a car, and drove myself to the campus. Tomorrow I'll do it all again, feeling less confident about my status as an adult, however, than I did back then.

Franco's first and only trip to my home came four years later. The day before we were to graduate she went home with me to attend my grandmother's funeral.

———

"What do you do if you have to go to the bathroom?" she asks me soon after we take off in the airplane.

"You go," I tell her.

"You mean there's a john?"

"Franco, haven't you ever been on a plane before?"

"No" she answers.

"So that's how come you decided to come along instead of going to graduation," I say.

"That's it."

Franco would rather be mistaken as opportunistic than too sympathetic.

My grandmother's house was a large, four-story farmhouse on fifty acres of land with a cow barn and several outbuildings.

"That's it?" Franco nearly exclaims as we turn off the pike and onto the private road to the farmhouse.

I'd been looking forward to impressing Franco. On the plane, instead of thinking about my grandmother who had just died, who had raised me and given me more than my fair share of the good things in life, I was imagining how impressed Franco would be when she saw where and how I'd grown up.

Except for Emma, the cook, and Roy, the handyman, Franco and I have the house to ourselves. Roy carries our bags into the house and asks if Franco will be staying in the guest room. I tell him no, that she will be staying with me, and Franco seems surprised. I don't know if it is the guest room that surprises her or staying with me.

We go to the kitchen to see Emma, and she tells us Wesley will arrive the next morning. Then we go out for a walk. Franco wants to climb up to the lookout I've described to her a dozen times.

"It must have felt like you owned the world," Franco sings out when she reaches the top of the oak tree. "Don't you ever worry that you might have already had it the best you're ever going to?"

I haven't told Franco about my parents because I want her to think that I had a dreamy childhood. On the ground below her, I laugh. She doesn't guess that it's a cover-up.

That night Franco and I sleep together in my big bed. It's a warm night so I suggest we sleep in the nude.

"Are you sure?" she asks.

"Yes," I say, "it will make me feel better." I don't mean I will be more comfortable.

Franco knows this and asks, "Won't this be sacrilegious?"

"Grandma wasn't religious," I answer.

The next morning Wesley arrives and sweeps Franco off her feet with his private boys' school manners.

"Your brother is almost as stunning as you," Franco says as we are dressing for the memorial service.

I'm grateful for the *almost*, and know it isn't true. Wesley was more refined in appearance and manner than I was. He and I were aware of the irony and we weren't uncomfortable about it, although we did see it made others uncomfortable, especially our parents. Our father tried to bully Wesley into being more spontaneous and expansive; our mother tried to shame me into being more reserved and retiring.

"They have everything else their way," I said to Wesley once. "Why should they have us the way they want?"

Wesley had come to me crying after father had yanked him around. "If I don't do what he says, he'll kill me," Wesley argued. He was truly afraid of Father.

"If he changes you he'll be killing you," I said, and wished that I hadn't because I could see I gave Wesley no way out of his dilemma. Either way he felt doomed. The day I learned that Wesley had killed himself this exchange of ours flashed into my mind, horrifying me. It stayed to haunt me for weeks.

Franco, Wesley, and I leave for the church before noon and are back from the cemetery before two. When we enter the house we are greeted by a noisy crowd of people and the over-whelming smell of flowers everywhere. I feel sick suddenly. Franco notices I'm looking peaked and suggests we go some-where and sit. On our way to the kitchen, away from all these people, we pass through the dining room where a large buf-fet is set.

Franco asks, "Who did all that?"

I have no idea, but Wesley overhears Franco's question and explains to her that it only took a couple of phone calls to the right people.

I see Franco's disappointment and wish he hadn't said that. Instead of feeling relief that Franco is cured of Wesley, I feel sad that she is because Wesley is my brother.

"Do you know all those people in there?" Franco asks me, once we've made it to the kitchen.

"I don't know any of them," I answer, sitting down on the back stairs.

"What's the story, Thad?"

"We weren't much of a family," I say. "We were familiar strangers like those people in there. They've been around me all my life, and I don't know any of them."

That night, after turning off the lights, I tell Franco that my mother and father were alcoholics. I tell her about the nights they would drink until they got drunk, then get Wesley and me out of bed to bully us. I tell her my mother would tear up the house and make me clean up the mess while my father and brother sat out on the back porch and drank.

"How old were you?"

"Young," I say.

"Your brother drank with your father?"

"He didn't want to, Franco. He felt he had to. And then he

would be up sick the rest of the night, and I would take care of him."

"Thad, that is terrible."

This is not the worst of my memories. I can't bring myself to tell Franco the worst, to repeat the words that were spoken on those nights, things that were said to embarrass and terrorize us. I don't even like to recall them privately. And, of course, I wouldn't tell anyone that I was glad—relieved—when my grandmother informed Wesley and me that our mother and father had been killed in an automobile accident.

After I've said all I can say and we are quiet for a while, Franco says, "I'm glad you told me all that."

"So you don't have to envy me anymore?"

"No, so you don't have to pretend."

Thursday, December 19
San Francisco to Woodbine

From my study window I watch Martha's car pull in the driveway. It's early. The fog is thick, but Martha's small red car is like a beacon of light.

"Thick as soup today," I say, opening the door. "I hope my plane takes off."

"It will," Martha says, as she steps in with a duffle bag hanging from her shoulder and a fish bowl in her arms.

"What's with the fish bowl?" I ask.

"I've decided rather than coming by to take care of Edna I'd move in for the duration."

"What about Ned?" I ask.

"He's going home to see his family for Christmas."

"Well, great! Would you like a cup of coffee before we hit the road?"

"I think we better go, Thad. It's almost seven-thirty."

Martha takes my suitcase out to her car while I say goodbye to Edna.

On our way, I stare out the car window at the foggy morning and imagine Edna, sitting on the other side of the front door. After a while, she'll give up and trot back to the kitchen to curl up in her bed under the table.

Martha turns to look at me several times. Finally she says, "Nothing's ever as difficult as you imagine it will be."

I thank her for that, and we drive on in silence.

Martha pulls around a yellow van, and when it is no more than a speck in her rearview mirror she blurts out, "Ned isn't going home for Christmas. He and I are separating." She goes on before I can react. "He met someone two months ago."

"Did you know?" I ask.

"No."

"Is it serious?"

"He says he's in love." Martha turns and gives me a sad smile.

"I'm sorry," I say, "and surprised."

"I'm not surprised," she says. "He's been acting strange for a while. I didn't want to ask why."

"You don't have to take care of Edna, you know. You could board her if you'd like to get out of town."

"No, I want to, Thad. Besides I have my work. No, I want to stay. I shouldn't have said anything."

"I'm glad you did."

"I was going to write and tell you, but it just came out."

"It's all right," I say. "It's not all right, but you know what I mean . . .oh, boy," I groan.

"Some Christmas, huh?"

"I'm so sorry, Martha."

"Oh, I'll be O.K. And maybe once he has her full time he'll change his mind."

"If that's what you want, I hope so."

"I don't know," Martha says, taking the turn into the airport.

"You don't have to come in with me," I say, as she heads for the parking lot.

"I want to," she answers.

When we get out of the car, Martha puts her arm around my shoulder and says, "Next time I think I'll fall in love with a woman."

"At least you haven't lost your sense of humor," I say, and we laugh.

At the gate, Martha reaches into her jacket pocket and takes out an envelope which she hands to me. "Open it on the plane," she says, and she gives me a hug.

I watch Martha walk away. She weaves her way successfully into a crowd until I cannot see her anymore. Then I turn around and look at the strangers who will board the plane with me.

Once on the plane, I settle into my seat at the window beside a woman my age who is in the aisle seat. Minutes later the plane taxis onto the runway, the engines roar, and my heart begins to pound. I'm on my way now, I think, as we lift off the ground. My back stiffens as the plane climbs. I don't relax again until we level off, and then I open Martha's note to me.

Dear Thad,

I might sound callous saying that I envy you. What I envy is not your battle but the feelings that make it one.

I hope you and Franco have a happy Christmas. I will be thinking of you.

Martha

Franco had been the one to take the initiative, approaching me in the first place, visiting me in the infirmary, then planting herself in the library, and later, inviting me to live with her. On Willis Street I waited for Franco to take the next step, the step everything prior had been leading up to. Weeks passed. Franco didn't say or do anything to indicate to me that she was interested in me except in the most casual and platonic way. I felt surprise and disappointment and, finally, desperation. One night, after Franco was settled in her bed, I went over to her. She looked up at me calmly, as though she had been expecting me. I opened my blouse, and when she didn't act as though she thought that was strange, I stood and took my skirt off.

I was living my dream, and it was almost more than I could bear. My hands shook as I undressed.

When our bodies touched, Franco and I both sighed, and then in embarrassment, we laughed. We pressed against one another, kissed with our mouths closed and then open. We wrapped our legs around one another, and when our eyes met, I could see that Franco was as eager for me as I was for her. I knew nothing could ever feel better than this. No one would ever matter more to me than she.

We didn't sleep that night. As soon as one of us started to fall asleep we were awakened by the touch of the other. In the morning when the sun came into our room, Franco nudged me out of her bed and I went to mine. We slept the whole day, missing our classes and meals, and by nightfall we were so starved I got dressed and went out to get us something to eat from Duffy's.

I returned to a stranger. Franco was dressed and at her desk with her nose in a book. She didn't glance up when I came in or when I put supper down on her desk.

"Are you all right?" I ask her.

"Of course, I am," she says. "I've got studying to do, don't you?"

"Sure."

"We can't repeat last night, Thad."

"What's that mean, Franco?"

"I've got to get more sleep."

"I didn't expect we'd—"

Franco cuts me off to say, "Maybe even separate quarters."

Separate quarters? What happened while I was out? I wonder. "Did someone come by while I was at Duffy's?" I ask Franco.

"This isn't about anyone else," she says, looking up at me.

"You seem different suddenly."

"I'm trying to read, Thad."

"Why are you?" I ask.

"Because that's why I'm here," she says gruffly.

I went out for a walk. I decided on my walk that I wouldn't push Franco for intimacy or answers. I didn't want to lose her. She was on scholarship, a serious student. She had to keep up her grades. That's what this was about and that's all it was about. She had panicked. I'll give her more time. I won't depend solely upon her for friendship. I'll make friends with the others in the rooming house. She'll come around, I told myself.

It was months later before Franco noticed that Alice and I had become friends. She asked me how I felt about Alice. I was intentionally vague. Franco tried not to appear concerned about Alice, but I saw that she was. It was working, I thought. But Franco and I left school after our sophomore year without any more intimacy, and I went home for the summer consoled only by our plans to continue as roommates our junior year.

Our first night back the following fall, Franco crawled into bed with me, and the next two years we were lovers. Franco seemed happier her senior year. I didn't want to think the reason was that she was going on to Johns Hopkins after graduation and I was going on to Columbia and therefore we would only be able to see one another on weekends. I didn't want to think that, but I did.

In the beginning we spent our weekends together in bed. Franco and I had gotten used to sleeping together, and we missed the physical contact. But by our second year of weekend visits sex alone didn't satisfy me. I wanted more. I wanted emotional intimacy with Franco. I felt out of touch with her. I wasn't a part of her world and she wouldn't talk about it with me. It was a painful disappointment to me that she wanted only a physical relationship. But I couldn't bring myself to tell her that I was unhappy. I didn't want to admit, even to myself, that we were headed in opposite directions, that we wanted very different things.

Franco's announcement months later that she'd decided to leave Hopkins, join Peter's lab, and live with me, did not convince me that things would improve because it had not even occurred to her to consult with me beforehand. This was not how I expected us to treat one another. And when Franco made it clear that her move back to New York was for professional reasons, not personal ones, I knew I couldn't stay.

I've been in California sixteen years now. Franco remained in New York until five years ago. I have been back many times to visit her, on holiday, when each of her parents died, and whenever she received an award. Franco has been out to see me once, seven years ago when she came to give a paper at Stanford. It was the only time in all the years I've known Franco that she seemed unhappy and tried, I think, to recapture some of the happiness we had once had with one another. It was not the right time for me.

I put her in my guest room, and soon after I'd gone to bed she came in to me. I pretended to be asleep until I saw she planned to get into bed with me.

"No, please don't," I said.

"Are you involved with someone?" she asked.

I didn't answer, and she went back to her room.

Two years later Franco left Peter's lab to teach at Woodbine, and I went to see her to suggest that I move back. It was her turn to turn me down.

––––––––––

"Are you all right?" the woman beside me asks.

"Yes," I answer, surprised by the interruption.

"You didn't seem to hear the stewardess."

"I was daydreaming."

"She asked if you wanted something to drink."

"No, thank you."

"Are you sure? You look like you could use a drink."

What's that look, I wonder. Sadness over things that never were?

As soon as the last row is served its drinks, the stewardess begins to collect the empty glasses from the first row. The pilot announces our approach to Albany, and my heart takes a sudden leap into my throat. The stewardess hurries down the aisle to check that all seats are in an upright position, that our seat belts are fastened. My heart is racing; I am perspiring. I stay seated when we land, to avoid the mad dash to get off the plane. Finally, the stewardess comes to see if I am riveted to my seat. I smile apologetically and wonder if anyone has ever refused to get off a plane and what is done to force them off.

Albany's small airport is a bustle of Christmas excitement. I rent a car. As soon as I am out of airport traffic, I look for a place to pull over. I park alongside the curb of a residential street, turn off my headlights and motor, and take a deep breath. No one has to know about these ten minutes. I won't have to account for them.

I push my seat all the way back and close my eyes. Oh, brother, I think, what is wrong with me? I start to shake and then I start to cry. The crying helps. I tell myself, *You're going to be all right*, and repeat, *You're going to be all right* to convince myself that I am. I open the car window and breathe in the cool night air, then pull the car seat forward and start the motor.

Snow darts at my windshield as I pick up speed on the highway. Twenty miles along the main route I turn off, on to the road that will take me into Woodbine. There are no street lights on this road and only an occasional house. I panic for a moment in the pitch black and turn on the car radio to some Christmas music. One of those Chipmunk songs is playing, so I switch to an all-night talk show.

My first trip to Baltimore to see Franco, I got lost somewhere on a labyrinth of thruway which came to an abrupt dead end. I suppose, now, that somehow I got onto a section of expressway that had not been completed. At the time, however, I was certain that I'd wandered into the "Twilight Zone."

When I finally got myself off the expressway and to a public phone, I called Franco and tried to describe to her where I was. She told me there wasn't an expressway anywhere near me, and I answered defensively, "I know what an expressway looks like and I just got off one."

"It doesn't matter, Thad. Just take Route 1 north. You'll either see signs for the hospital or for the Hopkins Sheraton. Follow them to—"

"Franco, you don't understand."

"What don't I understand?" she asks.

"I'm not just lost. I'm scared."

"What do you mean you're scared? Scared of what?"

"I don't know, but I can't get back in the car and drive."

"Yes, you can. You're only twenty minutes from here. Now pay attention to what I tell you."

"I can't," I tell her.

"You can't pay attention?"

"I'm scared, Franco."

"Thad, I can't come get you. I don't have a car."

"Take a taxi. I'll pay for it."

I can hear Franco groan, then she says, "O.K.," sounding disgusted. "Stay put, I'm coming."

I wait in my car with the doors locked and look in my rearview mirror at the headlights of cars coming toward me, praying that the next ones I see will be Franco's. Finally, a car pulls up behind mine and Franco gets out of it.

We don't speak on the way to her apartment, and once there, Franco acts as though nothing unusual has happened. I'm glad, because by now I am more embarrassed than frightened.

———————

The all-night talk show is taking calls from battered wives who, without exception, begin by defending their husbands. The psychologist points this out to one woman who then says, "He says it's my fault, that he wouldn't have to hit me if I behaved." I can't stand any more of this; I turn the radio off.

Minutes later my headlights light up the sign for Woodbine College, and I check my watch. It's seven-thirty. I take a right turn on Newman Street to pass by Nell's house.

There it is: M E R R Y   C H R I S T M A S, strung across Nell's porch. I park the car at her curb and start up the walk.

As I am pushing the buzzer I'm thinking, I shouldn't be doing this. I should go straight to Franco's. Then I hear Nell and see her on her way to the door. Too late now, I think.

"Oh, Lord, you're here!" she says.

"Yes, just," I answer.

"Come in."

"I can't stay," I say. "I'm due at Franco's in fifteen minutes. I just wanted to say hi."

"Well, come in to do that, before you let all the heat escape." Nell is wearing one of her mid-calf skirts which she has worn with knee socks and tennis shoes for as long as I have known her, and a red cardigan sweater which is stretched nearly to her knees.

"Were you calling to me or is someone here?" I ask, stomping snow off my feet on the foyer mat. "I don't want to barge in if you've got company."

"Neither," Nell says. "I was talking to myself."

"You were talking pretty loud to be talking to yourself."

"I'm getting hard of hearing," Nell says with a laugh, and asks me to take off my coat. "I'll call Franco and tell her you'll be late."

"No, don't! She'll be hurt I came here first."

"Nonsense. You'd be hurt, not Frances. Have a seat."

I sit down on the only chair in Nell's living room which doesn't have a pile of books or Christmas packages on it. In a far corner of the room the dining table is strewn with papers.

"What's all that?" I ask Nell when she returns.

"I'm writing a history of the college," she says, and adds, "Frances sounds relieved."

"That I've arrived? Or that I'm going to be late?"

"I didn't ask, but I suspect she's nervous about seeing you."

"How is she?" I ask.

"Let me get us something and then we'll talk."

Nell leaves the room and returns with hot tea.

"You'll notice some things," she says, handing me a cup. "She limps and her hands have a tremor. Nothing too obvious, but if you're sensitive to subtle disturbances you may be bothered by them."

Did I dare tell Nell my worst fear, that I would shudder or make a face at something peculiar about Franco?

"I've thought a great deal about you since Frances told me you would be coming." Nell didn't like Franco's nickname.

"What's in the tea?" I ask.

"You must have gotten mine," Nell says, and we exchange cups.

"I remember when you left for California I thought that was the last we'd see of you."

"And like a bad penny I keep turning up."

Nell laughs and says, "Not at all." She pulls her chair closer to me, leans forward in it with her forearms resting on her knees, and looks at me closely. I'm struck by how white and bushy her eyebrows have become. "You're doing very well from what I hear."

"I'm scared, Nell."

"Naw, you'll do fine."

"This has caused quite an upheaval in me."

"I can imagine."

"Losing something I never had."

"Don't look so far ahead. We haven't lost her yet."

"What did I do, Nell? Did I screw up?"

"No, I don't think you did."

"It haunts me."

"I wouldn't give you much for hindsight. It lacks the passionate present. You don't see things better when you're beyond them. When you're beyond a thing you're not the you you were."

"When you're about to lose something, you suddenly realize its value."

"So make the most of your awareness."

We drink our tea and talk about teaching, and when it is time for me to go, Nell puts on her cape and walks out to the car with me.

There was a point at which I wondered if Nell ever loved a woman, because she understood me so well. Now I think it's just as likely that I underestimated Nell's ability to understand the human heart.

"See you on Sunday," she says, as I get into the car.

"You will?"

"You two are having dinner here."

I roll down the car window to wave good-bye.

Driving from Newman over to Stuyvesant, where Franco lives, I must cross Willis Street. Instead of crossing it, I turn onto it. The street is dark, and I don't see the rooming house. I worry it has been torn down to build one of those modern dorms, or worse, a parking lot. Then I spot something familiar, an iron fence, and there, back farther from the road than the other buildings, is 73 Willis. The lamp over the door lights up the stone lintel and the snow falling around it. I stop for a moment to look and remember.

Most evenings we sat around the table after dinner and talked. One night the argument was over the use of animals in medical research. It was a lopsided debate: I was the only one on the side of the cats and dogs, and Franco, my good friend and ally, gave the opposition's best argument. I didn't know my subject nor my competition well enough, and I was close to tears when Franco did an about-face and took my side.

Afterward I thanked Franco for coming to my rescue. She said she hadn't done it to rescue me; she'd done it because she felt both sides of the issue had a point, and I hadn't made mine well enough.

I drive on, amused by my recollection and feeling at ease

for the first time since receiving Franco's letter. Some fear has lifted. Maybe because Nell said I would do fine.

Franco's house is a small cobblestone house. We used to pass it on our way home to Willis Street from classes, and if anyone had told us then that one day one of us would live in the house, we would have figured that would be me because I was the one drawn to it, the one who invented the sort of people I was sure must live in it.

Now, on the front walk, looking toward the house at the light in the one window, I am in no hurry to meet the person who lives here. I stand in the cold night air, my toes aching in my wet boots, and smell the smoke which tells me there is a fire burning inside, and still I do not move. It is my last moment before I see her, my last safe moment. One part of me holds me back and another, the greater force, pushes me onward.

I ring the doorbell. The door opens, and for an instant Franco and I stand still and look at one another. I see that she is just as I always picture her in my mind's eye—tall and slim, with thick, lively hair, bright blue eyes, and a warm smile. She is no surprise, and yet I am caught off guard by Franco, as if I had forgotten how beautiful and exciting she is.

I reach out to embrace her, and we hug in the open doorway. Then we step inside and close the door and hug again.

"You're here," she says, holding me close and then letting go.

I can't speak. My heart is once again in my throat.

"Oh, Thad," she says sweetly.

I swallow and say I'm sorry I'm late.

Franco reaches for me and hugs me again, strongly. "Stopping to gossip at a time like this," she says.

Franco takes my coat and hangs it on the rack at the door. I watch her. She has on a pair of soft grey flannels that fit snugly on her narrow hips. On top she's wearing a pink sweater, my favorite color on her. And instead of shoes, she has slipper moccasins on her feet. She is young and handsome and casual-looking.

We leave the hall and go into the living room. Franco's gait is awkward. She takes a seat in the easy chair, and I sit on the couch in front of the fire. She looks relaxed and happy.

"Were you worried?" she asks.

"Yes," I answer, taking a deep breath. She smiles.

"I'm so glad you're here. These last two days have been an eternity."

"How are you?"

"I'm O.K."

"You look wonderful."

"Would you like to get settled upstairs?"

"In a moment," I say. I look around the room and come back to Franco who has kept a steady gaze on me.

"What time did you leave?" she asks.

"We left the house about seven-thirty."

"We?"

"A friend took me to the airport."

Franco's cat jumps up on the couch, and I uncross my legs to make a lap for her, but Cleo prefers the arm of the couch to me.

"What's your friend's name?"

"Martha. She's also my ceramics teacher." I get up and stand in front of the fire.

"Close friend?" Franco asks.

"Fairly close. I've forgotten just what winter feels like," I say, turning to warm my fanny. I look around the room again and notice that Franco doesn't have a Christmas tree. "You don't have a tree," I say, surprised.

"I thought you and I would do that," Franco says.

"Oh, good. Well, I guess I better go get my suitcase out of the car."

Franco follows me to the front door. When I return to the house with my suitcase, she's gone from the hallway, and I start up the stairs with it.

Five years ago when I was here it was summer, and what I remember most was that it had a sun-baked smell. That smell has been replaced by the smell of balsam burning in the fireplace. The air was moist and outdoor sounds filled the house back then. Now the air is dry, the rooms quiet.

"Don't be too long," Franco hollers from the kitchen where she can hear me on the steps.

The guest room is a small dormer room with wallpaper on the ceiling and walls. I take my suitcase over to the bed and set it down on the quilt at the foot. Before opening my suitcase I step over to the narrow dresser and check the drawers. All but one of them are empty. The bottom drawer is filled with wrapping paper and ribbons. On top of the dresser there is a small tin box with needles and thread in it.

After putting my clothes in the dresser, I slide my empty suitcase under the bed and sit down on the mattress. On the wall opposite me is a wedding photograph of Franco's mother and father. I can't see it clearly from where I'm sitting but I remember it.

Oh, brother, I sigh as I knead the braided rug under my feet with my toes. I could crawl right into this bed.

"What's taking so long?" Franco hollers up the stairs.

I ask her to give me another minute. I pull myself up and go into the bathroom to wash my hands and brush my hair.

A bottle of Franco's cologne is on the shelf over the sink. I take the cap off it and smell it. Her terry cloth robe is on the back of the door. I touch the sleeve of it and am overcome by that old feeling that even when embracing Franco, she was slightly out of reach.

Downstairs, Franco is fixing us supper.

"Some things never change," I say, leaning against the back door in the kitchen.

Beyond this door is a yard with trees and rocks the size of boulders and an old pump and a shed. In the summer the shed is covered with red roses.

Franco puts a dish in the oven. "What never changes?" she asks.

"I could go right to bed without eating," I say. "And you are full of life and raring to go."

Franco straightens up and looks at me. Her eyes are sad. I wish I hadn't said that, I think. I wasn't making a point; I was just blabbing.

While our dinner warms in the oven we go into the living room and sit together on the couch. Franco takes my hand in hers and holds it. It's unusual for her to be this solemn.

"If I could trade places with you, Franco, I would."

"No!" she says, "don't say that. Tell me about yourself."

"What do you want to know?" I ask.

"Tell me something glamorous."

"Oh, brother, that's a hard one."

"Come on, you do all kinds of romantic things."

"Is that what you really think?"

"Of course I do."

"Well, you're wrong."

Franco looks at me hopefully. On the spot to charm her, I can't think of a single shining detail of my life.

"Don't look at me that way," I say.

"Come on, Thad."

"It's no use."

"Don't make such a thing of it."

"I'm sorry, Franco."

"You're too serious, Thad."

"I suppose I am," I say. I get up and go to the bookcase to take a record from it when Franco goes to the kitchen.

Moments later I hear a loud crash over the music and I run to the kitchen.

Our dinner is on the floor, and the baking dish it was in is smashed to smithereens. Franco looks up at me with a sheepish grin on her face.

"I hope you meant it when you said you could go to bed without eating? It was Nell's casserole," she adds.

"She'll understand," I say.

"I'm not telling her."

"What about the dish?"

"I've got one like it."

As long as we're having soup and sandwiches, Franco and I eat at the kitchen table. I tell Franco I prefer this to the dining room, and she gives me a look that says I can stop being polite.

"I mean it," I say. "This is perfect."

"You don't mean it," Franco barks, and I nearly choke on my sandwich.

We finish eating in silence, and I stay seated while Franco clears the table. I don't dare offer to help her. She stands at the sink, staring down into it, and says in a whisper, "I'm sorry I yelled at you."

When I say I understand she says, "You don't understand. Why do you think you do?"

"It's just an expression, Franco. I meant it was all right that you yelled."

"I don't want you to be nice."

"I was being honest."

"I'm afraid you'll be nice because I'm sick, and I don't want that."

"All right, I won't."

Franco leaves the dishes in the sink, and we go back to the living room. She stretches out on the couch; I sit down on the floor in front of the fire. The atmosphere is strained.

"O.K.," Franco says, "let's get it over with."

"Get what over with?" I ask.

"I know you want to ask me about it."

"If this is a good time."

"Cut it out, Thad! I mean it. I don't want you being careful. It makes me feel like I've got to be careful back."

I get up off the floor and take a seat in the easy chair where I can see Franco. Her jaw is set. She doesn't want to talk. I decide to tell her how I feel rather than ask her how she is.

"I felt like I'd been slugged when I got your letter, Franco. I've never been as upset over anything. I went to bed that night and when I woke up in the middle of the night, I knew something terrible was wrong but I didn't know what. I didn't want to know what. When I remembered you were sick, I wanted to believe it was a bad dream. When I realized it wasn't a dream, it was real, I was overcome by the sting of it."

"I wouldn't want to get that news from you."

How would Franco feel? I wonder. I would want her to feel as badly as I do, but in my heart of hearts I doubt that she would.

"If you can believe this, Thad, at times I'm almost glad I'm sick."

"Why do you suppose that is?" I ask.

"Could be I'm a lazy son-of-a-gun and it feels good to be off the hook."

"Not likely," I say.

"Some folks think we make ourselves sick in order to give ourselves a break."

"What do you think?"

"This is a rather radical solution. I think I would have picked something else."

"How do you feel, Franco?"

"Tired. I'm tired all the time. And frustrated because I can't do anything without exhausting myself."

"What's wrong with your leg?"

"It's actually my nervous system. Eventually the muscles will waste away. In my hands and arms, too. It's a bad deal."

"I hate this, Franco. I hate that this is happening to you."

"I quit teaching, Thad."

"Why? Too difficult to get around?"

"No. I didn't like it from the start, so why continue."

"I thought you liked it."

"I tried to, but I haven't got the patience to teach what I know. I like to look for the answers to things I don't know."

"Do you have any pain?" I ask, getting back to the subject.

"The spasms are sometimes painful."

"Do you take anything for them?"

"No."

"Why not?"

"I don't like being sedated."

"Are you scared?"

"I don't like what all this means. I didn't like not knowing either. Knowing is better, I guess."

"I wish this wasn't happening," I say.

Franco is quiet.

"Well, what's up for tomorrow?" I ask.

Franco looks surprised and relieved that I've dropped the subject for tonight. "I thought you might like to go for a walk, take a look at the campus."

"I would," I say. "It's been a long day, longer for you. I'm ready to go to bed if you are?"

"You go on. I'm going to stay down here a while longer."

That was an hour ago. Franco has not come up yet. I would like to know what she is doing down there. Do I dare go see? Would she mind if I checked on her?

I put on my robe and slippers and start quietly down the stairs. All the lights except one in the living room are off. I stand in the dark doorway between the hall and the living room. A fire is still going in the fireplace, and Franco is lying on the couch, reading a book. She has reading glasses on. I've never seen her in glasses.

She doesn't realize I am standing a couple of yards away. Should I step into the room and interrupt her, or stay put and watch her? I used to watch Franco studying when we were students together. I'd put down my book to gaze at her. She was never aware of me watching her, her concentration was so great.

What am I watching her for? Do I expect her to reveal herself to me in some way? Not expect, want.

Franco takes her glasses off, rubs her eyes, then rests her hands on her chest. Her eyes are closed. Is she sleeping or thinking? If she is thinking, what is she thinking? Afraid I will be heard leaving and climbing the stairs and accused of eavesdropping, I step into the living room.

Franco's eyes open. She looks up at me and smiles. I go over to her and sit on the arm of the couch. I put my hand on her head.

"You look very tired," I say. "I think you should come up now."

"Soon," she says.

I think of kissing Franco good-night, but don't.

"Good-night," I say.

"Good-night, Thad."

Back in bed, I imagine Franco on the couch. I like her in glasses.

Friday, December 20
Woodbine

The sun streams in the window and wakes me. I feel like I am inside a small golden box, or one of those Easter eggs with a pretty scene inside it. When my bare feet touch the floor, I'm surprised by the cold. I hurry to the bathroom. Franco's bedroom door is closed.

Downstairs, Cleo rubs up against my leg to let me know she's hungry. I find some food for her on a shelf in the cellar stairwell, then make coffee and walk around the house with my cup. The creaking of the floor boards, which is usually muffled by other sounds, is the only noise now and seems strangely amplified.

In Franco's office, the converted pantry, I look closely at the photographs on the wall over her work table. Franco is receiving an award or diploma in each of them. Peter is with Franco in one. His hand is touching her arm. I'm annoyed by the gesture. I leave the room, trying to forget Peter and old arguments, and enter the living room where I feel more comfortable. The books on the shelves, the antique lamp on the table, and the worn slip-covered chair and couch are not mine, but they are all familiar and dear to me. I feel at home in this room, and at the same time sadly out of place. I am a visitor after all. I run my hand along the back of the easy chair, touching the soft cotton. I had a fantasy, as a child, that stuffed armchairs were people and when I sat down in one, I sat down in someone's lap. I pick up a tiny ceramic cat from the table next to the chair and look at the plucky expression painted on its face, then set it down and go over to the bookcases. I am uncomfortable. The quiet has gotten to me. Alone in this room it is too easy to imagine it is some time in the future and I am truly alone.

I go upstairs to dress in long underwear, wool slacks, and a heavy sweater, then peek in on Franco. I'm not aware Cleo has been following me until I open Franco's door and she dashes in and leaps up on Franco's bed.

I step over to the big bed. Only Franco's head is visible, poking out from the comforter.

"I just want to let you know I'm going out," I say softly.

"I'm going to stay in bed a while longer," she answers.

"Are you hungry? I can bring something up for you."

"You won't walk around the campus without me, will you?"

"Not if you don't want me to."

"I don't."

"What about breakfast?" I ask, but Franco has closed her eyes and cuddled up with Cleo who is under the comforter with her now. I leave the two of them be.

It's cold and dry out, but the sun is bright. I sit on the big rock by the old pump in the backyard for half an hour before the sun's angle changes, and I'm shaded by a large maple tree.

I miss Edna and wonder how Martha is doing. I feel cut off from my ties. I'm surprised that at this moment Franco does not seem like one of them. Have I been on my own too long? Or am I doing this to protect myself? Minutes before I was agonizing because I felt our bond so strongly, and now I feel guilty because I'm missing others. How peculiar and confused and unsettled I am.

After shoveling Franco's front walk, I make a snowman in the yard, find two pine cones for eyes and a Yankee baseball cap, hanging on a nail in the shed, for a hat. When I step back to have a look at my snowman, I see Franco's face in the bay window. Once upon a time I wondered about my thrill at seeing her. I thought it was probably strange to feel as I do, but strangeness, I've learned, is beside the point.

Franco opens the front door and steps out in her robe and slippers.

"Why, it's the Iron Horse," she says in a joking manner.

"Who's the Iron Horse?" I ask.

"Lou Gehrig," she says.

I clump over to my snowman to take the baseball cap off his head.

"Oh, come now, leave it be. Why did you do that, Thad?"

"You know why," I say.

Franco turns and goes inside.

When I join Franco in the kitchen she says, "You're too melodramatic, Thad. This isn't the end of the world, just me."

"It doesn't do you justice to be so flippant," I say.

"Well, you're too damn serious."

"You hate that about me, don't you?"

"I don't hate anything about you," Franco says, as she pours batter onto her waffle iron. "It would be nice if you'd laugh once in a while," she adds.

"I do. Just because I don't find the same things funny that you do."

"If we don't laugh about this, Thad, we'll end up crying."

"Why not cry?" I ask. "What would be wrong with doing that?"

"I don't want to cry."

Franco lifts the top of the waffle iron and the waffle inside splits apart through its center, half of it sticking to the top of the waffle iron and the other half sticking to the bottom. There's nothing to do but begin again. I suggest that Franco pull the plug out of the wall and let the waffle iron cool down so she can wash it.

"I don't want to do it that way," she barks at me.

I watch Franco scrape away at the stuck waffle with a knife. When she accidentally drops the knife, she picks it up and heaves it across the room. Then she picks up the waffle iron, yanking the cord from the wall as she does, and she throws the waffle iron into the sink.

I hold my breath.

Next, Franco turns the faucet on full force and water splashes everywhere. She lifts the waffle iron out of the sink and throws it down a second time. If the sink were ceramic and not stainless steel she would have broken it.

"Hold on," I say, when Franco looks like she's about to do it a third time.

"This goddamn thing. I'm never going to use it again. Damnit to hell!" Franco kicks the cupboard.

"Calm down," I say to her, and she turns and gives me the evil eye.

"You can go to hell, too."

Who is this? What's going on?

Franco takes the waffle iron out of the sink and tosses it in the trash, then gets down on her hands and knees to sponge up the mess she's made on the floor. I want to help her, but I'm afraid to. She has some difficulty wiping up the floor and she bangs her fist against the cupboard. This is too much, I think. It's got to stop.

"If you're hungry you'll have to make something for yourself," Franco says bitterly. "I'm not doing anything more for anyone. I've had it!"

"I can see that," I say.

"You don't see anything," she says.

"I can see you've lost your temper, and I think you better get a grip on yourself before you get hurt."

"Stay out of my life, will you."

"Gladly," I answer, and I get up from the kitchen table and leave the room. Franco follows me out to the living room.

"Where are you going?" she asks.

"Out of your life," I answer, as I start for the stairs.

"Sit down."

"Why?"

Franco looks very worried. "Please sit down," she says.

I do. "What do you want, Franco?"

"I want you to appreciate what's going on."

"I do." *Appreciate* is an odd word to use, I think.

"No, you don't," Franco says. "You're appalled. I see it in your eyes."

"I can't help that."

"If you appreciated this, you wouldn't take it so damn personally."

"It's hard not to when you're yelling at me."

"This is what I want from you, Thad. I want you to let me handle this my way. If I want to joke about it, let me. If I want to throw things. . .I know you'd like me to react to this the way you would because that would make you comfortable, but I'm not you. I'm not going to be pathetic. I'm not going to cry about it. Do you understand?"

"I understand you think I'm pathetic."

"Oh, for crying out loud, I can't speak to you without offending you. If I'm going to have to watch out for your feelings—"

"You don't," I say, interrupting Franco before she can tell me what she will do. "Franco, I do appreciate what's happening to you. It's horrible. It's worse than horrible. You've got a right to react to it any way you want, and I will try not to be shocked. I won't be now."

"Come on back then, and I'll fix us some eggs. I didn't mean it about not doing anything for anyone."

"I'll fix breakfast," I say, and all the while I'm doing that I feel anxious, anxious about what's going on inside Franco and how it will next be expressed. I didn't expect her to be so explosive. And I sure didn't expect to be frightened by her.

Rather than feeling close to Franco as we head over to Woodbine Pond, near the place where we met, I feel as far from

her as I have ever felt. Whatever it is that always comes between us is here again, and I wonder if the gap is widening.
Worst of all would be to end up not even close friends. I'm
afraid of that death more than Franco's.

It isn't easy for Franco to trudge through the snow. She strug-
gles to do this alone, then takes my arm for support. The gulf
between us is narrowed somewhat by that.

"What is it?" I ask, when I see Franco smiling again.

"I was just imagining what I must have looked like."

"You don't have to imagine it; I can tell you. You looked like
a madwoman."

"You should have seen the look on your face."

This is close enough to an apology.

When we arrive at the pond, Franco gets down on the sled
we brought with us, and I pull her along on the frozen surface.
She is happy. For the time being we can be fooled by this wonderful fun into feeling we are eighteen-year-olds again. This is
how I first felt with Franco, reckless and carefree. We should
play more, I think.

Before leaving the pond, Franco brushes snow from its surface and calls me over to have a look. Peering through the
black, stone-hard ice, we see weeds and yellow leaves and a
fish frozen in place.

"I feel bad about the fish," I say.

"I think it's all beautiful," Franco says.

I pull the sled with Franco on it along the plowed roads,
home. It is late afternoon and growing dark. Franco left a light
on in the house, and I can see it from a distance. It is a wonderful sight.

"Do you think we would be better off if we saw things the
same?" I ask Franco.

"We'd see less," she says.

At home, Franco tells me Peter is stopping by after dinner.
We quickly lose the freewheeling joy of racing across the fro-

zen pond.

"Why is *he* stopping by?" I ask Franco.

"Because I invited him to," she answers defensively.

"When did you do that?"

"He called this morning while you were out."

"He's driving all the way up here to *stop by*?"

"I don't want to fight over this," Franco says, leaving me in the kitchen and going into her office. I follow her there.

"I only ask because it seems odd to me. And it's not like Peter has never been an issue with us. Isn't it understandable that I would want to know why he's coming all the way up here?"

"Are you through?" Franco asks, walking past me and out the door. I catch up with her in the living room.

"You said in your letter you didn't want to see anyone but me."

"Boy, you can go on."

"That's great, Franco. Avoid the issue and just insult me."

"It's happening all over again, isn't it?"

"I'm not sure I understand what you mean by *it*, but maybe we should sit down and talk about this calmly."

Franco sits down on the couch, and I take the easy chair.

"Peter called this morning to say that he's spending Christmas with his sister's family in Utica. I invited him to stop in here on his way there. I thought it would be fun for the three of us."

"You thought it would be fun for you."

"And you'll see to it that it's not."

"Why do you suppose he called to tell you his plans?"

"Maybe he wanted to see me. Is there something wrong with that?"

"I'd bet everything I have that you told him I was here."

"I probably did."

"Not probably. Of course you did."

"So you think you're the reason he's coming, not me?"

"I don't think his motive is friendship."

"What is it then?"

"When some people don't get what it is they want, they have to make sure no one else does either."

"That's what you think of Peter?"

"Yes."

"Well, he'll be here around eight. You don't need to join us if you don't want to."

The subject is dropped. Nothing is said about Peter over dinner. Because his arrival is imminent, however, he is foremost on our minds, and we are unable to talk about anything else. We eat in silence. I'm not looking forward to six more days of this roller coaster ride.

I'm upstairs taking a bath when Peter arrives. I have the bathroom door shut and the water running because I don't want to overhear their conversation. I planned to go to bed with a book when I finished my bath, but instead I look for clothes to put on and I go downstairs. Franco is surprised to see me.

Peter stands to shake my hand. He looks older than I expected him to look. Overweight and nearly bald, he's almost not recognizable to me. I'm sure I would pass right by him on the street.

"You look like your old self," Peter says to me. His focus, as always, is above my head.

"This *is* my old self," I say.

Peter asks me how I'm doing in California, and because he has only polite interest in me, he asks nothing more when I say I'm doing well.

"What brings you East?" he asks next, in his affected, welcome-aboard voice. Peter knows what brings me East, so what he's attempting with his question is to make light of my relationship with Franco.

"Love," I answer, and the room falls silent. What did Peter expect I'd say? Did he think I would be intimidated by him? That's it for me, I realize, when Peter turns to Franco and resumes the discussion they were having when I came into the room. I go to the kitchen to put coffee on and unwrap a fruitcake.

Seven years ago Franco was invited to Stanford to give a paper on a protein she had discovered. After the presentation, there was a question period, and most of the questions put to her were about Peter's work at the lab, not hers. When Franco revealed this to me, I said the audience must have been a bunch of jerks. She defended them, saying that since Peter was lord of the lab and she was only a serf, people were naturally more interested in him. But the following year Franco left the lab for a teaching appointment at Woodbine.

From the kitchen I hear Peter explaining the ramifications of Franco's discovery to her. Franco listens for a while and then tells Peter that she's kept up with the research. Peter doesn't seem to hear Franco's remark and continues to explain things to her which she knows.

"Peter!" Franco has to shout in order to get his attention. She has mine as well. "This disease has not affected my brain."

"I know that," he says.

I move to the door to look in on them. Peter has remained standing. Franco is now lying on the couch under the afghan.

"Then stop lecturing me like I'm a goddamn sophomore," Franco says.

"I'm just talking the way I always do."

"You said it!"

"Is something wrong?" Peter says, looking sincere.

"Damn you, Peter, you've always treated me like I was less, telling me what was what, as if I didn't know, hadn't in fact been the one to show you. You've been lying to yourself for so long you think you're the genius. You are always so quick to tell people that I work under your guidance and direction when you've been riding on my coattails since college."

"I don't know why you're saying this."

"Because it's the truth. And because I'm tired of going along with the charade to protect your ego."

"I guess this problem of yours has you pretty upset."

"Oh, shut up, Peter. This *problem* of mine hasn't made me irrational, much as you'd like to think it has. I don't give a hoot about the fame and fortune you reap from my research, but I'll be damned if I'll let you think you've buffaloed me, too. I'm going to die with my self-respect, Peter, so you can take your act somewhere else."

Holy shit, I think, and I step into the living room. Ironically, I can't enjoy this stunning blow to Peter because I'm feeling sorry for him. He stands horror-stricken, his jaw lax. As soon as he notices me, he straightens and stiffens up.

"Well, I guess I'll be on my way," he says.

"I'll walk you to the door," I say.

At the door Peter says, "Take good care of her." Any other time that kind of charge from Peter would have annoyed me.

"I will," I say.

"And of yourself," he adds, looking at that spot somewhere above and to the right of my forehead.

I put my arms around Peter and give him a hug which touches him too deeply. He hurries away without his boots.

Franco is staring at the fire when I return to her. I go to the kitchen and get the fruitcake I was going to serve and two cups of coffee.

"I'm not drinking coffee," Franco says, and she asks me for some brandy instead.

I put another log on the fire and sit in the easy chair. Franco raises her glass and says, "Here's to *your* health, Thad."

"I never know what to expect of you," I say, and Franco smiles. "How come you never said that to him before?"

"I felt sorry for him."

"Why? He always had it better than you."

"No, he didn't. Maybe to others it looked like he did, but not to himself and not to me. I loved what I was doing. Peter's been running scared all his life, keeping up the pretense."

"What a pair we are. Tonight you finally let Peter have it like I wished you'd done on a dozen other occasions, and I feel sorry for the poor bastard."

"Nice language, Thad."

"Look who's talking. I haven't heard you say so many *god-*

damns as you have today."

"It's been a trying day. I was surprised you came down after your bath."

"I saw you were. And speaking of that, taking my bath tonight I remembered that I had my own temper tantrum the day after I got your letter. I'm sorry I reacted to you the way I did this morning. I should have understood."

Franco chokes on her brandy and I start to laugh, thinking it's a reaction to my apology. When I see it is not, that she is in trouble, I jump up alarmed. Oh, Christ, I think, pulling her arms up over her head. This thing is really happening to her.

As soon as Franco is O.K., I suggest that we go on up to bed.

"You go on," she says. "I'll be up in a little while."

"What is it, Franco?"

"Well, to be honest, Thad, I have this funny way of getting up the stairs."

"And you don't want me to see you."

"I'd rather you didn't."

"You go on then, and I'll stay down here and clean up."

"No, you'll peek; I know you, Thad."

"I love you too much to do that, Franco."

"Come on," she says, "I'll use you instead."

We climb the stairs together, Franco leaning on me for balance and support as she grapples with her right leg. She doesn't see how this breaks my heart because she is concentrating so completely on what she is doing. Halfway up, Franco sits down on a step to rest and surprises me by asking me if I have a lover.

"I have a social life," I answer.

"You go on," she says. "Go on down and clean up. I can make it on my own."

In the hallway below I look back and see Franco lift herself up, one step at a time, on her fanny.

Half an hour later, I am in my bed and she is in hers. A hallway separates us. I'm not sure why this is, so I climb out of bed and walk across the hall to Franco's room. She is sitting up in bed with a low lamp on.

I sit down on her bed in the dim light, and she takes hold of my hand.

"I want to say something."

"What's that?" she asks me.

"I don't know."

"Do you want to get our tree tomorrow?" Franco asks.

"Yes, let's do."

"We're going to be all right, Thad."

"I hope so," I say.

Franco leans toward me and kisses me good-night. It is the first time in many years that I have felt her lips on mine.

Saturday, December 21
Woodbine

The sound of a snowplow wakes me in the morning. I roll over in bed, feeling hung over from a dream. In it I kept taking wrong turns on my way somewhere, getting lost in places that I'd never been and unable to understand anyone who gave me directions.

Franco is up before me, I realize when I hear the bath water running. I close my eyes and drift back into a light sleep; this time I dream that Edna speaks to me. It seems perfectly natural that she can do this, and when I wake and realize it was only a dream, I'm disappointed.

I get up and go to the bathroom. Franco has returned to her room and shut her door. The bathroom is steamy and smells of her cologne. I fill the tub and ease down into the hot water. From where I rest, I can see out the bathroom window to the top branches of a tree where a flight of birds is perched. It is snowing out, a wet, sleety snow, and I wonder why the birds aren't on a lower branch, in closer to the trunk where they might be sheltered from the elements.

Back in my room, I look out and see that the snowplow has piled snow in front of Franco's drive. I dress to go out and shovel it so we can go get our Christmas tree.

Franco calls me in to breakfast just as I finish clearing away the heavy snow.

"We've got a problem," she says to me in the front hallway. "Peg just called, and I've got to go see her." Before I can ask why, Franco says, "She's in trouble, Thad."

"What kind of trouble?"

"She wasn't specific about it, but she sounded bad."

"I don't think we should go. You don't look up to it."

"I'm fine," she says.

I tell myself I'm not going to argue with Franco over this.

"I'm going with or without you, Thad."

"How do you plan to go without me?" I ask.

"I'll take the train."

"You're a stubborn cuss," I say to Franco in the car, on our way to her sister's.

"We'll get our Christmas tree tomorrow," Franco says.

"It's not the Christmas tree I'm concerned about. By the way, does Peg know?"

"No."

"Are you going to tell her?"

"We'll see how it goes."

"Do you have any idea what's wrong with her?" I ask, and Franco only sighs. "I hope she isn't crying wolf."

Franco says she thinks it has something to do with Peg and Dan separating.

"When did they do that?" I ask.

"When Peg joined A.A."

"Where is Dan?" I ask.

"No one knows. He pushed her around one night, and she got a court order that said he had to leave her alone. A few days later he tried to break into the folks' place, but Peg had changed the locks."

"Is *that* where I'm taking you?"

Franco nods her head. "They had to sell their house last year to pay debts, then evict the couple renting the folks' place in order to have someplace to live."

"Things have gotten worse."

"I thought they were getting better for Peg, but now I don't know."

"What's her problem today?"

"I think she went off the wagon."

"You mean she sounded drunk on the phone?"

"Yes."

I don't tell Franco how I dread facing that ordeal, that I still have nightmares about my parents. It is probably a good thing the roads are slippery and the driving difficult because this forces me to give it my complete attention.

The three-hour drive to Newark takes us five hours, and we don't arrive until three in the afternoon. Already it feels like a long day.

The driveway has not been shoveled, so I park the car in the road in front of the Coles' house. Franco and I start up the walk, or where we figure the walkway is, since it has not been shoveled either.

"I've got a feeling the place has gone to seed," Franco says.

"We'll try to keep our sense of humor about it, eh?"

"Peg never was much of a housekeeper."

We ring the front doorbell and wait.

"Maybe it's not working," Franco says, and we go around back.

The window is broken out of the back door. Beyond it is the kitchen. Peg is lying on the floor in the kitchen. Franco reaches in through the hole in the pane and opens the door. Even with this ventilation the room smells very bad. It is hard not to gag. Franco cannot believe one person could make such a mess, then lie in it. I've seen it all before; it's the nightmare of my early childhood: cabinet doors hanging open, drawers pulled out, a week's worth of dishes in the sink, crusted with food, more dried and sticky food dripping down cabinet fronts to the floor, a pool of gunk on the floor, and a half-dressed woman lying in her own vomit.

Franco cannot go near her sister to see if Peg is alive or dead. I see the look on Franco's face that I felt as a child in my gut. It is aversion, which will be replaced by guilt later when recalling her reaction to someone she loves.

I step over to Peg and lift her up into a sitting position on the floor. She opens her eyes, looks blankly at me, and closes them again. "Let's go," I say. "*Ladies Home Journal* will be here to interview you in an hour."

Franco scoots a chair over, and together we lift Peg up and onto it. Peg sits slouched over with her head swaying.

"God, she smells awful," Franco says, and she goes and gets the sink sponge.

"What are you doing?" Peg asks in a peculiar groan, which is almost more than I can bear to remember, and Franco wipes the vomit from her sister's cheek and hair.

"I'm going to try to get her upstairs and into the tub," I say.

It is next to impossible to do this because Peg is uncooperative. It annoys her that someone else's will is forcing her to move. She keeps repeating, "Leave me alone, I want to sleep." On the stairs she manages to pull from my grasp and elbow me in the eye.

Franco helps her undress, and Peg gets herself into the tub because she thinks she will be left alone to sleep there. I leave the two sisters, and as I head downstairs I can hear Franco bawling Peg out. I think to myself, that never works on someone who is feeling sorry for herself.

I'm feeling a touch of self-pity myself, as I return to the kitchen. I cleaned too many messes like this before I was ten years old.

Twice while cleaning the kitchen I rush to the bathroom downstairs to throw up in the toilet, and afterward glimpse at myself in the mirror. My eye is nearly swollen shut.

There has to be a radio somewhere, I think, and eventually I locate one in the living room. I turn it on to a station playing Christmas carols. On my way back to the kitchen, I call up the stairs to Franco to make certain she is doing all right. She doesn't answer, and I race upstairs in a panic.

Franco is sitting on the bathroom floor against a wall, staring at her sister in the tub. Franco's clothes are wet, and she looks dejected. The bathroom floor is also wet. I can see there's been a struggle.

"What's happened?" I ask Franco.

"She won't let me get near her," Franco says, sounding forlorn.

Peg isn't thrilled about me bathing her either, but I do it. When she is settled in bed I call Alcoholics Anonymous and am promised a woman will come by at six o'clock to relieve us.

At six, sharp, Lorraine arrives. She takes one look at my eye and says, "No one told me about that."

"She's not violent," I say. "It was an accident. I got an elbow in the eye when I was helping her to bed."

"Looks like more than an elbow to me."

I feel too much resentment will build if I stay in the bedroom with Franco and Lorraine, so I wait downstairs for Franco to say good-bye to Peg and join me. Instead, Lorraine comes down and asks if there is any food in the house.

"Not much," I say. "But you're not going to feed her, are you?"

"I was thinking about myself," she says. "I haven't eaten dinner."

I apologize and offer to go out and get Lorraine something. As I am putting my coat on I ask her, "How do you do it?"

"I've got to," she says. "It's what keeps me sober."

"My parents were alcoholics," I volunteer.

"So were mine," she says.

"One night they ran off the road and killed themselves."

"I'm sorry," says Lorraine.

"I wasn't," I answer, admitting this to someone for the first time. My confession doesn't seem to surprise Lorraine, let alone shock her.

"You can get me a burger and fries and two large Cokes."

"How long will you stay here?" I ask her.

"Till morning, then we'll go to a meeting."

I like being out of the house. Things that would ordinarily not seem wholesome to me, do: neon signs, a movie marquee, the golden arches. I am even able to get myself a burger and eat it in the parking lot.

Franco is waiting for me in the kitchen when I get back to the house. She tells me I can leave Lorraine's dinner on the kitchen counter and we can go.

"Will you ever forgive me?" Franco asks as we get into the car.

"It wasn't your elbow," I say.

It is eight o'clock. The temperature outside has dropped enough to turn wet, slick roads into icy surfaces. I feel tired and dirty and can't wait to get home and take a bath.

"She said she was anxious and she sounded a little drunk, not like she was. If I'd known it was going to be . . ."

"We still would have come, take it from me."

"Do you think she'd been drinking for days?" Franco asks.

"A few, at least, from the looks of the kitchen and the empty bottles."

"She didn't know why I was there. She didn't remember calling me."

"I'm not surprised."

"I asked her why she was drinking again, and she said she had the flu. I asked her if Dan had called or tried to see her, and she said she wasn't sure about that. Then I thought, if she hadn't remembered speaking to me on the phone, it was pointless to be asking her all those questions. So I stopped and just sat there."

"I'm sorry, Franco."

"And while I was sitting there I kept thinking how much it would hurt Mom to see Peg like this. Peg was special to Mom. Mom was forty when Peg was born. It was no favor to Peg, being so much younger than the rest of us. We had established our allegiances to one another. Peg was the baby, the messy kid, the one who laughed at dopey things, who we didn't care to have around or listen to. Mom was her only friend in the family. Peg started drinking hard when Mom died." Franco rests her head back against the car seat.

"I'm sorry," I say again, feeling sorry for Franco, not Peg. She is dying, I think. Peg is only sick; Franco is dying. Today was hard on Franco. She began it looking worn-out. Now her voice is weak and her spirit diminished.

Life seems especially cruel when one of its staunchest members dies in their prime. This is the staggering reality in San Francisco nowadays. Two friends of mine died this year from AIDS, and at the funerals of both I had a moment of smugness because I'm a lesbian. It didn't occur to me to think about other killers. Franco has some of the look of those men. The hollow eyes and the slow, tired walk.

At home Franco has an episode of muscle spasms in both her arms. I build a fire in her room because the house is cold and help her into bed. I'm exhausted and thin-skinned and I feel undeserving to be the healthy one. On the verge of tears, I get body oil from the bathroom to massage Franco's arms. At first, Franco has her arms tucked tightly to her body and resists my straightening them out. I am aware as I touch her just how deeply I love her. If only God would use me to heal her. I pray for this, and a thought comes to me—a thought that is not mine—that something better is at work. I hear my mind answer back that I don't want that. I know what that means. It means I will lose her. Then Franco's body seems to let go of all its tension. Her face relaxes, her hand opens, and I feel an extraordinary sense of well-being. I must remember this, I tell myself. There will come a time when I will have to let go of Franco and I will need to remember my joy at seeing Franco at ease.

Without taking the bath I promised myself on the drive home, I hurry out of my clothes and into my bed, feeling relieved that Franco is sleeping, pleased that I was able to help her, and sensing a foreboding loneliness.

Sunday, December 22
Woodbine

It is the coldest day yet. The windows are frosted on the inside as well as the outside. I lie on my side in bed and stare at the small windowpane where the sunlight is refracted by the frost. I imagine myself huddled under a pile of animal furs in a large, horse-drawn sleigh with a fir tree tied down in back of my seat. My horse's breathing sounds like a loud bellows, and the bells, fastened to the leather straps against her withers, jingle as she canters along. I cannot see beyond this picture to the place where we are headed. I see only me and the horse and the sleigh and the tree and the white which is all around, and I feel a perfect joy.

In the bathroom, sometime later, I examine my eye. It is swollen completely shut. I should have thought to put some ice on it last night.

Downstairs, I make an ice pack and lie down on the couch with it on my eye, hoping to return to my horse-drawn sleigh. But I cannot go back there because I am too eager to get on with the day.

"Well, one of us looks better," I say, taking a breakfast tray in to Franco.

"Thad, your eye is awful! Nell is going to think I slugged you."

I'd forgotten we had a date with Nell, and I'm crestfallen.

"You don't want to go, do you?" Franco asks.

"Not really," I answer.

"We have a full day until then," Franco says reassuringly, and perhaps because I go along with her and decide to be cheerful, she feels it's then safe to express her sadness over Peg, but I'm not up to that.

"Let's not talk about her," I say, and Franco stops short.

"It's not like you to be unsympathetic," she says.

"I'm not," I say, but Franco looks unconvinced, so I explain that my attitude has less to do with Peg than my parents.

Franco lets it go, perhaps as reluctant to get into the subject of my upbringing as I am reluctant to talk about yesterday. While she eats her breakfast, I sit at the foot of her bed and lean against one of the four posters.

"I envied you, having all those sisters," I say after a while. "I used to listen to you complain about being thrown together with no privacy or quiet, and I would think, how wonderful it would be to share a room with someone, to have sisters to talk to about things you couldn't speak to anyone else about."

"We shared, all right," Franco says. "We didn't have anything that we didn't have to share. Every toy I ever played with was missing something by the time it got to me—an eye if it was a doll, a wheel if it was a truck. I envied you in that big house with rooms to roam in and a yard that went on forever with trees to climb and even a pond to swim in."

"All by myself," I add.

"What about Wesley?"

"Wesley and I didn't play together. We weren't allowed to because he was a boy. Franco, sometimes we didn't even talk to one another for days."

"My favorite time of day was walking home from school by myself so I wouldn't have to talk to anyone and I could think a thought through. I'd go home the long way, through the woods that scared Ellen and Louise. Even in bed at night it was impossible to do that because there were three, sometimes four of us in that room. I couldn't even pretend in the dark that I was alone. I could hear the breathing of the others."

"Would you have traded with me, Franco? Had my childhood instead of yours?"

Franco is quiet for a moment, and then she says, "No, I guess not."

"Well, there you have it. I would have traded with you."

"Is that your test?"

"Yes. Don't you agree it's a good one?"

"No. Almost everyone will choose the known over the unknown no matter how bad the known is."

"What about you?" I ask. "What do you choose?"

Franco is quiet again. Then her eyes cloud over as though she might cry, and she says, "I'm a tough customer."

Instead of responding *Amen* to that, I say nothing.

It was unusual when Franco talked about her family. I don't recall a time she did when someone hadn't initiated the discussion by asking her a direct question. But today is different. Franco's frame of mind or her circumstance has made it desirable, perhaps necessary, that she talk about her past.

She begins before we leave the house. On my way downstairs I happen to glance in on her, standing in front of the bathroom mirror, and without turning to me, but continuing to look at herself in the mirror, she says, "Ellen used to practice her French in front of the bathroom mirror." I feel something more is coming and I wait. I don't want to walk away until I'm excused with some gesture. "I thought she looked silly doing it," Franco says, "but now I think maybe I envied her." With that, Franco turns and smiles, and we go downstairs to dress to go out.

Then as Franco is buttoning up her peacoat she says, "The first time I saw Patrick in his Navy uniform I was dazzled. I think that's when I realized that to be wonderful you had to be a boy."

It is at this moment that I am aware of something odd about Franco—she is reminiscing. My reaction to it is equally odd;

I wish she wouldn't. Since I have always enjoyed hearing about someone's past, and longed to hear more about Franco's, I suspect my attitude has to do with an unwillingness to accept the circumstance which leads Franco to do this.

In the car, she gazes out the window on her side as I drive. I feel her slip away, then hear her say, "He left all his clothes at home when he joined, so I went and cleaned out his closet. They were the only hand-me-downs I ever loved."

"Your mother let you wear your brother's clothes?" I ask, not because I am surprised or question her mother's judgment, but because I don't like this feeling that it doesn't matter whether or not I'm listening to her.

"Mom never paid much attention to what we wore," Franco answers me. "Patrick has a small scar on his cheek that is my teeth marks," Franco goes on happily. Her attitude is also strange because I would expect these memories to make her somber. "I was accused of biting him, but I remember the incident clearly, and that I'd meant to kiss him when my passion ran wild. Every time I see that little scar I want to tell him the truth. Only something stops me."

I am about to ask Franco what it is that stops her when she answers, not me but herself. "He'd think I was silly to bring it up."

That said, Franco seems to have taken care of something. She sits back and resumes looking out the window, and now she seems to see what she is looking at. She even comments on the ice hanging from the tree branches.

But when I pull into a gas station to fill the car, she drifts away again, and as we are leaving she says, "One summer we were all packed in the Pontiac, on our way to Pines Lake, and we had to stop at a gas station to let some of us out to go to the bathroom. When we drove away we left Louise standing at one of the gas pumps. We were down the road several miles before anybody noticed she wasn't with us."

"Poor kid," I say.

"I always felt I was to blame for the oversight because I was in charge of Louise. Ellen was in charge of me, and I was in charge of Louise. And Louise would have been in charge of Peg if there hadn't been so many years between them." Franco is quiet for a moment, then, "Ellen didn't mind being Mother's helper, but I did. I didn't want to be responsible for someone else's kid, even if it was my own sister."

"I understand that," I say, and Franco turns and smiles at me. Her smile doesn't suit the mood of what she's been saying, and it occurs to me maybe she isn't aware she's speaking aloud. How very odd. I don't like this. It makes me think she's nuts and I'm invisible.

I'm glad when we arrive at our destination and we can get out of the car and do something.

The Christmas tree lot is located on an acre of land between a woods and an apple orchard. It is one of those lots where you cut down your own tree. I tell Franco I don't want to do that, and she looks at me like I'm a big dope.

"Isn't there another lot where they're already cut?" I ask her.

Sounding more than a little perturbed, Franco asks the apple farmer if he will cut a tree for us, but before he can answer her, I pull Franco aside and say, "That's no good. We'll still have to pick it out, and I'll see it alive."

"Boy, you're being a baby about this," she says, and she turns back to the farmer and asks him if he knows of a lot where the trees are already cut. "My friend is sentimental about cutting down a live tree," she says, to be sure he doesn't misjudge her.

The farmer points to a barn on his property and tells us, "There's plenty of them in there."

Franco and I are the only ones in the huge barn.

"I don't see the difference!" she shouts, although we are standing right next to one another. "These were alive once!"

"It's not a matter of alive or dead," I say in a whisper. "It's killing them that bothers me."

"The word is *harvesting*," Franco says with emphasis.

"It's killing just the same," I answer, "and if you don't button up, you're going to ruin these for me, too."

With a wave of her hand, Franco lets me know what she thinks of my sentimentality, and we begin our search among the various trees: long-needle pine, spruce, and fir. The balsam fir smells the strongest and is my favorite. Franco agrees and we stick to them. I hold first one and then another up for her to check for a straight trunk and uniform thickness. When we decide on the same one, we turn to one another stunned.

"Can it be?" I ask.

"Our first agreement," Franco says, but then she thinks a moment and says, "No, we agreed that *Catcher In The Rye* was our favorite book."

"It wasn't mine," I say. "I only said so to prevent an argument."

"It wasn't my favorite either; I said so because you did."

I lift our tree onto the roof of the car. Getting it to the car, Franco and I exhibited the kind of teamwork we always have. As Franco started to move ahead, I started to back up. As she started right, I started left. I reversed my direction to get in step with her, she did the same, and once again we were pulling against one another. Finally, Franco said, "You better do this alone."

On our way home, Franco remembers we need milk, and we stop at a grocery store to get some. I've tied the tree to the roof with a rope I passed through the window openings. Now, in order to open our doors and get out of the car, we have to undo the rope.

"I knew that would be a problem," Franco says.

"Then why did you let me do it?" I ask.

"Are you kidding?" she says.

Just ahead of us in line in the grocery store is a pregnant mother with her teen-age daughter. Once we are on our way again, Franco says, "That was me back there."

"What was you?" I ask.

"The girl in the store just now."

"What about her?" I ask.

"She was embarrassed by her mother the way I used to be in public. People would ask Mom when she was due, and I would be mortified that strangers knew my mom was still doing it with my dad. She was only forty years old—my age. Of course she was doing it."

"I liked your mom," I say, recalling an experience of my own with Mary Cole.

Once Franco and I are home, having carried the tree into the house, put it in its stand in front of the living room window, and paused to catch our breath, Franco asks me what it was I liked about her mother. This is even more remarkable than Franco volunteering information about her family.

"There was a lot to like," I answer.

Franco lies down on the couch and pulls the afghan up over her, while I build a fire in the fireplace.

"One time when we were in Newark visiting your family," I say, "I got up before anyone, or thought I had, and I went downstairs to get some coffee. Your mother was in the kitchen. When I walked in, in my robe and slippers, she glanced up and waved in that off-handed way of hers, like I was one of the gang she saw every morning, not surprised or disappointed that I wasn't one of her kids. She handed me a glass of orange juice without asking me if I wanted any, and a cup of coffee, and when she took the bacon off the stove, she broke a piece in half, gave me one end and ate the other herself. Then she sat down at the table with me. When she caught me looking at the edge of linoleum by the sink where it was warped and cracked, she said she was thinking about taking up the linoleum and putting down some of those new-fangled squares that are self sticking. I told her I'd just take up the linoleum and sand the wood floor, and she gave me that look you give me all the time."

"What look is that?"

"The look you gave me when I said I didn't want to cut down

our Christmas tree. Then, in a voice of experience, your mom said, 'Oh my, don't you know you'd get crumbs between every board.' "

"We didn't have a vacuum," Franco says.

"I figured that."

"So, then what?" Franco asks.

"That's it," I say.

"That's it?"

"Yes."

"What's so special about that? I thought you were going to tell me why you liked my mom."

"Franco, I did! Weren't you listening?"

"Yes, I was listening, and you didn't say."

"Because she made me feel like I was one of you!"

"Oh . . . it was that important to you?"

"What have I been telling you?"

"Boy, it's hard to understand why you would want to be one of us."

"Damn, you can be dense sometimes," I say, getting up off the floor to string the lights on our tree.

Franco watches me from the couch. I expect her to tell me exactly what and how to do it, but instead she continues to reminisce aloud.

"Back at the house after Dad's funeral, when Mom and I were in the kitchen alone, she told me that Dad had been so afraid that she would die first and leave him alone, that she never told him how scared she was of being left."

I stop stringing lights in order to watch and listen to Franco.

"She told him she'd be all right so he could die in peace, but she told me she didn't think she could survive without him."

"Why do you sound angry about that?"

"Because I was angry, Thad. I was angry because she put on me what she wouldn't put on him."

"Maybe she needed to tell someone the truth."

"Damnit, Thad. She was always burdening the wrong person. She knew I would worry about her. She wanted me to.

So, I did, but not without resentment."

"You're awfully hard on her," I say, as I go back to stringing the lights on the tree.

Franco is quiet for a long while and then she says, "Did I ever tell you she knew about us?"

"Your mom?" I ask.

"When I was at Hopkins I wrote her a letter and told her I was thinking of leaving there to return to New York and be with you."

"You mean to be with Peter."

"No, I don't mean that. Peter had nothing to do with my personal life."

"You told me your decision to come to New York was professional, not personal."

"That's not so. It was entirely personal."

I let go of the string of lights I'm holding. "That's not at all what you said then."

"Thad, you've always been so sure you weren't going to get what you wanted, you didn't see it when it was right in front of your face."

"No, no," I argue, but suddenly I feel sickened by this, and confused. Is it possible I misunderstood Franco, or is she rewriting that piece of our history to make it seem that I, and not she, am to blame for our separation? "Franco, you insisted it was professional."

"I insisted my relationship with Peter was professional, not my moving to New York. Anyway, Mom wrote back to me that she'd always known you were the special person in my life and she thought you would be good for me."

"*Anyway*? Franco, if I misunderstood you back then . . . why didn't you say something? When you saw I was leaving . . . didn't it bother you to lose me over a misunderstanding?"

"Yes, it bothered me a lot. But I wasn't going to beg you to stay."

"You wouldn't have had to."

"Well, whatever, it's the past."

"No, not whatever, how can you brush it aside that easily? Everything would have been different if—"

"Everything wouldn't have been different, Thad. It wasn't that one misunderstanding that kept us apart."

I sit down on the floor and try to sort things out in my mind: What was truly said and by whom. What actually happened and why.

"Thad, it doesn't matter."

"Of course it matters," I say.

"Let go of it, Thad."

"I can't let go of it. If what you're saying is true, then everything changes."

"Nothing changes. That was that. This is this."

"This changes," I say. "This now! Us!"

"I wish I hadn't brought it up."

"And how come you haven't before?"

"Thad, if we were meant to live together, then we would have. We would have gotten along better, misunderstood one another less, and not let differences get in the way."

"You mean to tell me you think our lives are predetermined?"

"Perhaps."

"I don't buy it."

"Don't then. Make yourself miserable."

I stop arguing and think about that. "Oh, Jesus, have I done that? Have I expected things not to work out, so of course, they didn't?"

"No," Franco answers me. "It wasn't your fault. It's never one person's fault. It's the combination and the circumstances and maybe fate."

"I can't talk about this anymore. It's making me heartsick."

"Good. Put some music on and let's decorate our tree."

"Did your mother really say I'd be good for you?"

"She said she *thought* you would be good for me."

"I don't want to hear another critical thing about her, Franco. Your mother was a genius."

"I'm glad you liked her."

I get up and put a Christmas album on, and struggle against its peaceful message. I am angry because Franco didn't push me to understand her better. Halfway through the album, it occurs to me again that maybe I didn't misunderstand Franco. Maybe she needs to think I did. Whatever the truth is, Franco is right about one thing: it's too late to debate it.

I go back to stringing the lights on the tree. When that is done, I get the box of tree ornaments down from the attic crawl space, and while I hang the ornaments on the tree, Franco goes through her photo albums, looking for photos to give me. I would like to have some of those pictures of us as young women, but that the time has come for Franco to pass things on is such a painful reality, I cannot bear to watch her do it. She is braver than I, I think, as I hang a papier-mâché butterfly on a branch of our tree.

Every now and then Franco asks me if I would like a picture of this or that. I say yes, and I hear her pull the photo off the page. After an unusually long pause, I turn to see what Franco is up to, and I see that she is crying. I leave what I am doing and go to her. I put the album aside and take Franco into my arms.

———

It worried me that Franco didn't cry at her mother's funeral. Then days after I'd returned to California, she called me in a panic saying, "Something awful is happening, Thad."

"What is it, Franco?"

"I can't get a hold of myself. I haven't been able to go to work or see anyone because I can't stop crying."

"That's wonderful."

"Thad, didn't you hear me?"

"Yes, I heard you. You need to cry, Franco."

———

"I don't want to die, Thad."

"Of course you don't," I say.

"I'm not ready to die."

"You never will be," I say, and Franco pulls away from my arms to look at me. "You never will be," I repeat, "because you love life too much."

"That's right," she says, looking startled by the simple truth. The thought that she might never be ready to die seems to put Franco at ease. "Do you think it would be just as hard whenever?" she asks me.

"I think it would seem too soon whenever."

"I guess you're right. I hadn't thought of that."

"What happened just now that made you cry?" I ask.

"I was looking at a picture of me sunburned. Remember how sunburned I got on Fire Island? And, I thought, I'll probably never get sunburned again. And suddenly it was so very important. It's crazy, I know."

"No, it's not crazy."

————————

Two summers after we graduated, Franco and I spent a week on Fire Island. I'd skinny-dipped in Torch Lake, Michigan, too many times to count. As a child I used to bathe in the lake. But, Franco, to my surprise, had never skinny-dipped in her life.

No one is on the beach when I stand up, roll my bathing suit off me, and run naked to the ocean. Looking back from the water, I see Franco, standing startled beside our beach towels.

"Come on!" I holler to her.

She comes in for a swim with her suit on, and I coax her into taking it off in the water. As soon as she does, a strong wave yanks it from her and carries it back to the beach.

"Now what?" Franco asks me.

"I guess you'll have to stay in here forever," I say, laughing at her.

"I can't get out of here with nothing on," she says, crouched down in the water.

"Oh, Franco, you're not having any fun?" I leap into the air with the next wave, and Franco grabs my arm and pulls me down.

"Thaddy! Everything you've got is showing!"

With the next wave I show Franco just how brave I can be when she is not. I throw my arms around her and shout as loud as I can, "I love you!"

———————

"I wanted so to get a tan like you," Franco says, pointing out a picture of the two of us on Fire Island. "Do you see how beautiful you were?"

"I've always felt you were the beautiful one," I say.

"You've always been wrong."

"When are you going to tell your family that you're sick?" I ask.

"When the time is right," Franco answers. "In other words, I'm not sure. I'm not sure about much of anything."

"I wouldn't believe you if you said you were."

"Except one thing."

"What's that?"

"I don't want to go to Nell's tonight."

"We could cancel," I say.

"We could, except I know she's looking forward to this visit with you."

"Then I better get busy and finish the tree," I say, getting up from the couch.

When the last ornament is on the tree, I pull a chair over to it, stand on the chair, and put the star on top. It is a paper star made of a double thickness which allows me to slip it down over the top branch.

Franco and I turn out the lights in the room and sit down on the couch together to gaze at the red and green and blue lights, twinkling on our tree. The only white light shines through the pinholes in the paper star on top.

We are quiet for a long time before Franco says, "I don't know how we're going to leave it to go out."

"We can't go back and we don't want to go forward. We're in a helluva predicament," I say, and Franco looks at me with more intensity than I have ever felt from someone's gaze. It is not a hard look, but a thorough one, powerful and compelling and extraordinarily intimate. And then we kiss, and what we knew would be difficult now seems impossible. But which one of us will call Nell and tell her we'd rather be alone tonight? Neither of us can do that, so, without saying more than a word or two to one another, we get up from the couch, put on our coats, and start out of the house.

Franco does not take her eyes off me in the car. I feel her desire everywhere her eyes touch me, and I wonder how on earth we are going to eat a dinner and make casual conversation with Nell.

We arrive at Nell's a half hour late, but Nell isn't one to care about such details. She greets us warmly, and we step inside. Her place is immaculate.

"Where is it all?" I ask, stunned.

"Don't open any closets," she warns.

We have a good laugh and settle into chairs in the living room.

Nell thinks Franco looks better than the last time she saw her, and she gives me credit for Franco's improvement. When I say, "In spite of me would be closer to the truth," Nell walks the fence like a pro.

"Frances has always blossomed with a challenge."

"And how do you think Thad looks?" Franco asks Nell.

"It's hard as hell to ignore an eye like that!" Nell says, and we laugh again. We might have preferred to stay at home tonight, but this is also good, to be laughing with another old friend.

"I banged into an open cupboard," I say.

"She's lying," Franco says. "I slugged her."

"You're both lying," Nell says, and Franco and I look at one another, amazed.

"We went to see Peg yesterday," Franco begins, then goes on to explain what happened.

Afterward Nell looks at me. I expect her to comment on my eye or the cause of it, but instead she says, "I got it in the eye once. I was standing behind the target, and the target ducked."

"Who was the target?" I ask.

"The man I was with. It came from out of nowhere, and so quickly I never knew who swung or why. I was knocked out cold. Later I was told a tale I couldn't believe, so I told folks who asked that I got a tennis ball in the eye. You ought to know, Thad, that if you want people to believe a story, you've got to make it interesting. A cupboard just isn't very interesting."

Franco enjoys Nell ribbing me. She grins and pulls her legs up to her chest to squeeze herself. I am feeling grateful for the small surprises in life, coming here with a reluctant spirit and delighting in the good time I'm having.

Over dinner, Nell tells Franco and me that teaching had not been her career choice, but her parents' choice for her. She tells us she had wanted to go into the theater. Her parents had opposed her, and in her day it was difficult for women to buck their parents. I realize as she is speaking that the thing that would have made Nell successful on the stage is what made her successful in the classroom, a talent to inspire belief in an idea.

"Is there something else you might have done?" Nell asks me with her next breath.

"I would have married Franco," I answer.

"A woman can be a wife and a teacher," Nell reminds me.

"I think she had in mind being a husband, not a wife," Franco pipes in. It is Nell who asks Franco to explain that.

"Thad never gave me the impression she was willing to play second fiddle."

"Would that have been necessary?" Nell asks, her tone becoming serious for the first time.

"I think that was one of our dilemmas," Franco answers as seriously.

I'm surprised that Franco has thought about our impasse enough to have formed an opinion about it. I'm glad that she has, though. It is a compensation of sorts to know that it mattered enough for her to think about it.

"But if it had been our only dilemma we would have found a way around it," Franco adds. I don't have to pursue this because Nell does.

"Was there a greater one?" she asks.

"Yes," Franco answers. "Our mothers. Thad and I wanted from one another what our mothers didn't give us, and that put us in conflict."

I am beyond surprise. I am fascinated.

"For Thad it was bonding. For me it was escape."

"You're right!" I say, and Franco turns to me.

"Why are you surprised?" she asks.

"I underestimated you," I say, the words spilling out before their meaning sinks in.

"Every time she came close, I backed up. She would reach out to seize, and I would thrash to be free. We have been warring this way for more then twenty years."

"Is there any way it might have been different?" Nell asks Franco.

"If one of us had been more courageous," Franco answers.

"Yes," Nell acknowledges. "That is always the answer."

I am humbled by this exchange. I have always believed that because I advanced I was the courageous one, the willing one, the open mind. And, because Franco pulled back she was the coward, the unwilling one, the closed mind. S*he* fought *me*, and if *she* would just stop *we* would be fine. What *I* wanted and desired was what one *should* want and desire. And, furthermore, I thought about all this while she did not, because she mattered more to me than I mattered to her.

On the way home in the car I ask Franco how long she has understood all the things she said, and she tells me she did early on. I hear myself say, if she understood our dilemma early on, why didn't she behave differently. I realize I am doing this because I want to continue to put the blame on Franco. And

I have to ask myself why I am afraid to take responsibility. I have no other answer than I'd rather be a victim than the cause of my own pain.

While we were having dinner at Nell's, a snowplow nearly buried our car on the street, and I had to shovel us out. Now, back at home, I'm unwilling to give up my coat to the hall rack because I am chilled through. Franco insists I take a bath first.

"Hand it over," she says to me when I step into the bathroom, my coat still buttoned around me.

"I don't know if I can," I say, reluctant to strip down. Finally, I am able to do that. As I sink into the hot water, Franco starts out of the bathroom, then stops in the open doorway and stands with her hands in her pockets just as she stood in the doorway of Drake Infirmary.

"I think I'll recover," I say.

"Do you know, Thad, the first time I saw you I thought, here is Veronica, Archie's dream girl, everyone's dream girl."

I have never thought of myself as anyone's dream girl. I am not unattractive, but I am not glamorous either.

"And I said to myself, somehow I've got to win her over. But how am I going to do that? I can't put on a Navy uniform and be her hero, and I don't have any feminine wiles. I'm just a person. Someone she thought was a boy and might have been disappointed to discover was not."

"How did you know I thought you were a boy?" I ask her.

"I saw how surprised you were when I spoke to you."

"Well, you turned out to be a girl, and I wasn't disappointed!"

Franco picks my clothes up off the bathroom floor and leaves.

When I finish my bath, I clean the tub and fill it for her. I go to tell Franco it is her turn, and I see she has gone to bed.

"Did you change your mind?" I ask her.

"Thad," she says in a steady, calm voice, "come to bed."

Perhaps I shouldn't be surprised, but I am.

I take off my robe and slide into bed with her. Franco's breasts touch mine, and I am thrilled by my awareness of her womanliness. Her legs and mine stretch to meet and entwine and I feel my heart beat hard and my skin tingle. I want to crawl over her and under her and press into her and become a part of her. Her mouth, open and hungry for love, finds mine the same. It is a long, long time since we were this way together: straightforward, aggressive, immodest, and happy. The relief, the joy, the amazement are so great that for a while we cannot make love, because making love requires some self-restraint, a place to begin. We need to squeeze and slide and bend and roll. In time, I am able to breathe deeply and relax so that Franco and I can do what we mean to do, to win and be won in the most intimate way. Whatever this precarious life is about, and whoever we truly are, Franco and I met, fell in love, and are together again. Her touch, her gaze, her responses are what I desire. I don't know how I have lived with less. If I had never known her sweetness and her passion, I might have lived with less, in ignorance and satisfaction. But knowing her and living with less, I have felt thin and uninspired. At the peak of my pleasure I have the knowledge that I will lose what I love. I am acutely aware there will come a time when touch will be impossible. And at that moment of pain and pleasure, Franco says, "Well, here we are again," in a waggish tone, smiling brightly at me. And I am overcome with something more powerful than my desire for Franco. It is my love of her. For all the pain loves carries with it, I am glad that I love her. It is the best thing I have done.

Franco falls asleep before me, and I lie beside her, admiring her. An arm of hers is stretched out, relaxed, elegant, and I can see the pulse in her narrow wrist. She will always be alive to me, I realize. She is etched on my brain, or in my heart, or wherever it is one soul's impression is left on another.

Monday, December 23
Woodbine

I roll over in bed and reach out for Franco. My hand finds a vacant place where she was and I panic. Then I hear music, a record playing on the stereo downstairs, and I get out of bed and go down to see what Franco is up to.

She is in the living room dancing with Cleo. Her back is to me. She has on her terry cloth robe and her slippers. Her hair is still mussed. Cleo is resting, front paws and chin on Franco's shoulder, looking in my direction but not giving me away. I am a witness to a private moment. I don't want to be discovered and the moment to dissolve. Franco's dancing is a kind of rocking back and forth, left foot, right foot, in time with the music. It is early. It is not yet light outside, and the lights on the Christmas tree glimmer in the shadowy room. The music is gay, and the atmosphere partylike. It is delightfully odd.

Then Franco turns, and I see she is smiling. She doesn't stop dancing when she notices me; her smile broadens, and she continues dancing until the song ends. Then she gives Cleo a kiss and sets her down.

"I'm teaching Cleo to dance," she says.

"She's a quick study."

"At first she insisted she lead so we tried it that way, but her legs are too short."

"You're a lovely pair," I say.

"Yes, we think so."

I put my arms around Franco and pull her close to me. We kiss and look at one another.

"I feel wonderful today," Franco says.

"I love you," I say.

"Were you upset I got up?"

"No, but I did panic for just a moment when I woke and you were gone."

"I couldn't sleep. I was too happy. Coffee's on and rolls are in the oven."

Franco and I sit down on the floor by our tree to drink our coffee and eat a light breakfast.

"Tell me about Martha," she says.

"Martha?"

"Yes, Martha."

"What about Martha?"

"She's more than your ceramics teacher if she's taking care of Edna."

"She's also a friend," I say.

"How close a friend?"

"Not intimate. Is that what you're getting at? Franco, I don't have a lover, if that's what you want to know."

"If Martha isn't then I guess you don't."

"And why is that?"

"Because your lover would be the one taking care of Edna."

"Yes, I see what you mean. Why didn't you just ask me if I had a lover?"

"I did. You said you had a social life. It sounded like a yes."

"I don't have a lover. I do engage in sex. Not with Martha."

"No one serious?"

"No one serious."

"Was there someone else when you moved to California?"

"I'm not sure what you mean."

"Was someone else the reason you left?"

"My God, no! I was in love with you. Why would you think that?"

"You left. I was sure you didn't care about me any more."

A loud siren interrupts us, and I use the interruption to think about Franco's remark, to wonder about this Franco who was unsure of herself, or my love.

"There was only one thing stronger than my love for you, Franco, and that was my need to feel loved. I couldn't stay because I was afraid my relationship with you was becoming like the one with my mother. I was afraid I loved you more than you loved me, and I was sure that would kill me. I wish I'd told you that then, but maybe I didn't understand it enough. I doubt that I did . . . enough to explain it to someone else."

We hear a second siren. This one is closer, and I get up and look out the window.

"Can't tell where it is," I say.

"I asked you here because I needed to find out if you still loved me," Franco says, and I sit back down. "I needed to know you did."

"Why is that, Franco?"

"I needed someone to care that I'm going to die. If no one cared, it would be hard."

"Oh, Franco, of course I care."

"This way I feel my life mattered because I mattered to you. I would feel pointless if I hadn't made a difference to anyone."

"You've made a difference to many."

"No. Only you."

"You can't believe that. You don't even know how many lives you've touched and changed."

"That's true about you, Thad. Not me. I haven't had that much to do with people. I don't let people get to know me as you do. I've been busy with my career. And now I think the career thing doesn't matter much."

"Of course it matters. Do you think you're here just to share yourself with others? That was what women were told for ages to keep them slaves at home and slaves of others. You're here to become something, not just be. You've got a brain to use. And you've used yours. My God, Franco, you discovered something no one knew existed. You opened a door to who knows where. I envy that kind of contribution."

A third siren shrieks in the distance.

"And you've also mattered to people," I say. "You've mattered to your family and your friends. To Peg, to Nell, to Peter—I hate to admit—and to others I don't know and you don't need to tell me."

"How to you?" Franco asks.

It is astounding to me that she needs to ask this, that it is not obvious to her. "Franco, you make me feel alive. And good about myself. Your loving me has made me feel worthy. That someone as remarkable as you looks at me the way you do. . ."

"Don't say any more or I won't believe you."

I put my arms around Franco. She is more unveiled than I ever imagined she would allow herself to be. Now, more than needing to be a winner in the world, since worldly matters are rather beside the point, she is telling me she needs to know her life counted in a personal way. And she is willing to unveil herself completely and ask if she is loved. At the same time that she seems childlike to me in her naturalness and nakedness, she is also way beyond me. She is the teacher or mother engaged in things I've hardly begun to look at. And I am a bit in awe of her. We pull away, and she smiles at me. No one smiles as much as she. Her situation does not make her pathetic or even unhappy.

"I wonder about that fire," she says, having had enough of serious talk. Before I can voice a similar concern about the nearness of the fire, there is a loud knock at the back door. "That will be our turkey," Franco says. "I arranged to have groceries delivered this morning."

There are more groceries than space to put them, and the turkey looks to be about eighteen pounds.

"Who's coming for Christmas dinner?" I ask, jokingly, but I'm struck with the possibility that my joke may be right on target.

"I like leftovers," Franco says.

"You'll be eating them on Easter Sunday," I say with relief.

Franco clears a shelf in the refrigerator and asks the delivery boy to put the turkey there for her. Then she asks him if he knows where the fire is, and he says, "On Newman Street."

Franco and I have the same sudden fear which is confirmed by what the boy says next.

"I think it's that place with the Merry Christmas sign."

"No!" I cry.

Franco swings around to phone Nell. She is dialing Nell's number when the delivery boy says, "You know that old lady that lives there?"

"Yes, we do," I say.

"No answer," Franco says to me.

"I'm going to get dressed."

"Is that all, ma'am?"

"That's all," Franco says.

The deliver boy waits for Franco to give him a tip.

Franco just looks at him. Ordinarily I don't think she would have been this dense, but her concern about Nell diverted Franco's attention.

I see Franco's wallet on the counter and take out a couple of dollars. The delivery boy stares down at the bills I put in his hand, obviously disappointed.

"I'm going up to get some clothes on," I say.

"Me, too," Franco says.

The boy puts the bills in his pocket and leaves.

Franco and I see smoke and can smell the fire three blocks from Newman Street, where traffic is being detoured. We can't drive any closer, so I park the car in the first spot I see, and we walk over to Newman.

Four fire engines are lined up in front of the houses on Nell's end of the block. At first we cannot see which house is on fire because there is so much smoke. Then we see smoke coming from the windows of the house next to Nell's.

"It's not Nell's," Franco says with such gladness it has a strange effect on me.

Why can't Franco be as lucky as Nell, I think.

A few yards down the block, we are able to see Nell, wrapped in a blanket, standing with others across the street from her house. We holler to her, and she looks around but cannot find us in the crowd.

"It's us," I say, finally making my way to her side. "Thank God it's not your house!" Franco says, joining us.

Nell gives Franco a peculiar glance and introduces us to Irene DePaul. It is Irene's house that is burning. Franco looks ashamed and apologizes, and Irene says she understands.

I put my arm around Franco and whisper, "You took the words right out of my mouth."

Three young children are huddled around Irene DePaul. Their ages look to be five, eight, and perhaps twelve. The youngest, a girl, stares at the house on fire, eyes sparkling. Her eight-year-old brother understands a little better what's happening, and asks his mother, "Can I go get my Mr. T before he burns up?"

"No! Stupid!" his brother says.

"Don't call me that."

"Don't be stupid, then."

"Andrew and Will, please stop that."

"Is everything going to burn up?" the youngest now asks.

Irene pulls her daughter Bess in close to her and does not answer.

"I'm freezing, Mom."

I look at who spoke and notice that Will and his brother have on only pajamas and slippers. Of course he's freezing. I start to take off my coat when Nell gives up her blanket. Irene wraps the blanket around both boys, but Andrew will have no part in sharing a blanket with his baby brother.

"He can have it," Andrew says, "I'm not cold."

"Andrew, I don't want you getting sick. Will, share it with him."

Once the two are under the blanket together they begin to squirm and Irene pats the head of the older brother. The squirming ceases.

I tell Franco I'm going back to the house to get some things and ask her if she wants to stay or come with me. She stays.

I take the extra blanket off my bed and Franco's, throw mittens, hats, and wool scarves in a pillowcase, then make some tea and pour it into a thermos.

When I return to the scene, I see the crowd has thinned out. The DePauls are sitting on folding chairs on the sidewalk, watching the firemen struggle to keep the houses on both sides of theirs from catching on fire. The DePaul's house is lost. Charred holes where windows were expose a charred indoors.

"Where are we going to sleep?" Will asks his mom. "Are we going to be like those street people?"

"No."

"What about Santa Claus?" Will goes on. "He won't be able to bring us anything because we don't have a house."

Bess starts to cry, and Andrew complains, "I'm hungry, Mom. Give me some money and I'll go to Duffy's."

"Not now," she says, comforting Bess. "Santa will find us, sweetheart. He doesn't need a house."

"But, Mom, I'm hungry now."

"I don't have my purse, Andrew. I'll have to go to the bank."

"Why didn't you bring your purse?"

"Because I had more important things to think of, like getting you out safe."

"You didn't have to get me. I got myself."

Irene realizes I've been listening to all this, and she looks up at me. "He's hungry," she says. "My husband used to get itchy when he was hungry."

I give the boy some money and tell Irene, "Later," when she looks at me chagrined.

Franco has been listening and watching and now pulls me aside.

"Let's give them our turkey, what do you say?"

"What are they going to do with a turkey and no oven to cook it in?" I say, and the moment the words are out of my mouth I realize what I've done. Franco looks at me earnestly, imploring me to give in to her desire.

"We could," she says, and then, "we should."

"Tonight?" I ask her.

"Why not," she says cheerfully. "Let's do it. It'll be good for all of us."

"Oh, Franco," I groan.

"I want to do it, Thad."

"I know you do," I say, knowing I've lost and hoping her invitation will be turned down. It's not.

Franco and I stand with the DePauls and Nell and watch the drama drain out of this tragedy for those not personally affected. The crowd disperses, the news reporters leave with the fire trucks, and only an inspector and one fireman remain. Nell is told her house is safe to return to, and she and the DePaul family start across the street.

Irene looks back in my direction and thanks me for the invitation to dinner, and something tears inside me. Do I see Franco in Irene's face? Or me, losing Franco? We share some sadness, I feel. The sadness of defeat? Defeated by something not at our command, a sad reminder that we do not have absolute control of our lives. Not so superior, after all, only human. With this tearing I feel a release, and I think I know it. It is freedom from pretense, freedom to be who I am, a chance for personal integrity to champion in me.

At home, Franco and I polish the cherry table, put a basket of holly in the center and candles on either side, and set seven places.

I prepare the turkey while Franco sits at the kitchen table and talks to me. I am not especially generous, but I don't begrudge what we are doing for others tonight because I am getting something myself. An easier, open Franco sits and talks to me. It feels like a gift, although I know I am simply here as it is happening. Franco isn't doing this for me.

"Thad," she says, "do you think a mother's life, because she has children, is more worthwhile?"

"I think society has tried to get women to believe that."

"You don't agree, then?"

"I don't feel like an authority on the subject."

"Tell me what you think."

"I think no life is complete, Franco. And some motherless women blame childlessness for feelings of incompleteness."

"And you don't think that's it?"

"I know mothers who also feel incomplete and blame having children for being unable to grow as individuals."

"Did you ever want children, Thad?"

"I've thought it would be nice to be pregnant and to have a baby, but I never wanted to raise a child."

"I think it would be wonderful to watch a child grow, to take part in the various stages, to play with a child and teach it a few things."

"I didn't know that about you, Franco."

"Yes, it's true. I never told anyone because I didn't want it used against me. Do you think I'd feel differently about dying if I had a child? I do."

"I don't know, Franco. If you think you would, you probably would. Chances are I wouldn't be here if you had a child and that makes me sad."

"Why sad?"

"Isn't it obvious?"

"Don't feel badly, Thad. I'm just thinking things through."

"I know you are." I put the turkey in the oven. "To think I used to beg you to tell me how you feel."

"Why are you smiling?"

"Because it's a good one on me."

"Don't you want me to talk to you about these things?"

"I do, Franco, but they don't all go down so easily."

"You can take it."

"I hope to God I can."

Just before company arrives, Franco comes to me and says, "I have these two things I was going to give to you for Christmas that I've decided to give to the two younger ones."

"Well, if they're suitable for them, maybe it's no great loss."

"Thanks for being a sport."

"I'm not giving Andrew your present," I say.

"What should we do about him?"

"You've got a thought; I can see it in your eyes."

"What about the sled, Thad?"

"Our sled?"

"The one and only."

"Ah, Franco."

"I won't then," she says.

"No, go ahead, Franco."

"No, I won't," she says. "I'll give it to you."

"No, give it to him. It will hurt me either way."

Franco puts her arms around me, and we are embracing when our company arrives. We jump apart when we hear the doorbell. Franco and I aren't ashamed of who we are or how we love, but we do know we are different, and that makes us vulnerable. When we do the common, ordinary things everyone desires and needs, we are looked upon differently. When we hold hands in public, when we talk about our personal lives with friends, when we go home to visit our families or attend a social event where spouses are invited and expected, when we do these and countless other things which most people take for granted as natural expressions of self, we are conscious of our difference. It does not mean that we feel badly about ourselves or others, but only that we are self-conscious. So, as I go to the door with Franco to greet our guests, I am feeling embarrassed and wish I were not.

We spend no time at all visiting before we sit down to eat because everyone is hungry. At the table, Bess sits on a telephone book between her brothers. Her hair is in braids, held by red rubber bands which came off carrots from Nell's refrigerator. Will has on a pair of jeans which are too big for him and must be held up with an Indian beaded belt that Nell gave him. And Andrew, also wearing clothes from the church box, has on Nell's sneakers because there were no shoes his size. I see he is self-conscious about wearing girls's shoes, and I would bet the farm that when Andrew is an old man and his memory of this Christmas is no longer sharp, he will still recall the sneakers and his embarrassment wearing them. Irene sits with Nell, across the table from her children. She looks tired.

For the first part of the meal the kids tell Franco and me how they spent the afternoon. It sounds like an adventure—being interviewed by the local television station, seeing themselves on TV, Bess and Will taking naps in Nell's bedroom with the fish tank and being read to from *Moby Dick*, while Irene and Andrew were at the church getting clothes for everyone.

By the time we are having seconds, Nell is entertaining us with one of her half-truths, a story about the time she went to a Deans' Conference and shared a hotel room with the Dean from Brown. She was asleep when her roommate arrived and she didn't hear anyone come in. Then she woke around midnight needing to go to the bathroom, got out of bed, and when she reached the open door to the bathroom, saw a man standing at the toilet.

"I ducked into the closet because there wasn't enough time to reach the bed," she tells us. "And, whatever I decided to do, I had to go to the bathroom first. I planned to slip out of the closet when he got back in bed, and as I started to do this, an umbrella, hanging in the closet, whacked me in the head and I let out a howl. The light in the room went on, and I heard someone yell, 'What the hell's going on?'

"I grabbed the umbrella to defend myself.

" 'Who are you?' he asked.

" 'That's what I'd like to know,' I said.

"The hotel apologized but blamed me for registering as Dean H. Glass instead of Dean Helen Glass. They moved me to the President of Mount Holyoke's room, but the next day I found my Dean of Brown and asked him if he snored. He said no one had complained that he did, so I asked him if he would mind if I returned to his room since the dean from Holyoke did."

Franco and Irene laugh, and because their mother is laughing, Bess and Will also laugh. Andrew remains quiet. When asked why, he says he doesn't believe Nell's story.

"Which part don't you believe?" Nell asks him.

I can see she is serious. Maybe she wants to know so she can improve her story.

Andrew looks afraid to say, afraid, perhaps, the adults will laugh at him.

"Sometimes I bend the truth a bit to make a better story," Nell tells Andrew. Then she takes her attention off him.

After dinner, Franco invites the children to put on their jackets and go out to the shed, "Where," she tells them, "you might see something you'd like to have."

They turn to their mother.

"One small thing each," she says. "And no fighting over anything or you know what will happen."

The three race for the door.

I hear Franco tell Andrew the sled is for him. Then I turn my attention back to the table and catch a spirit sagging. One moment Irene seemed almost playful; this next she looks forlorn.

"Do you have any children?" she asks me.

"No, I don't," I answer.

"Didn't you want any?"

"No."

"I wish I'd been smart like you," she says.

"It wasn't smartness," I say. "I'm a lesbian."

"Better yet," Irene says, and she looks at Franco, who returned to the conversation in time to hear me say lesbian, or perhaps when I did. Franco nods her head. "No one told me I could do that," Irene says matter-of-factly. Not knowing her it's hard to say if she's a comic or naive. "I sure would have chosen it if they had," she says, and we all laugh.

Franco is the first to quiet down. Any other time she would have been the last. Nell leans close to Franco, and they say a few words. Then Franco, looking at me, says, "I'm feeling a little tired."

"Why don't you go on up?" I say, but Franco says she would rather lie down on the couch, and Nell goes with her into the living room while Irene and I clear the table.

"Is your friend very sick?" Irene asks me in the kitchen.

I put the plates I'm carrying down on the counter and answer, "Yes."

"You've been watching her closely."

"I'm sure I have."

"What's wrong with her?"

Will bursts into the kitchen from the back door, wearing the Yankee baseball cap. "Look what I got, Mom!"

"That's wonderful," Irene says, but with less enthusiasm than he'd hoped for. Disappointed, Will runs back out to his brother and sister.

"It's not possible to have a private moment with anyone," Irene says to me when he's gone.

"If I were you, I think I'd make some time."

"And who would take care of them?"

"I'd find another mother in the same predicament," I say, and I go back out to the dining room to bring in the last of our dinner dishes. When I return to the kitchen, I ask Irene what she is going to do now.

"We're going to go to Ohio where my brother lives," she says. "He asked us there last year when my husband died, but I wanted to stay here. Now we haven't a choice."

"I always look at a second chance as something meant to be," I say, hoping I don't sound patronizing.

"What will you do if your friend dies?" Irene asks me.

"I don't know," I answer. "What did you do?"

"I had the kids."

"Do you do anything with other women?" I ask.

"No," she answers.

"Don't let your children isolate you," I say.

"What do you teach?" Irene asks, maybe wanting the attention off her.

"English Literature," I say.

"I always wanted to go to college."

"There are lots of good schools in Ohio," I say.

When the children return from outside, Franco tells Bess and Will the gifts under the Christmas tree are for them, and their mother allows them to be opened. Inside Will's package is a lamb carved out of wood and hand-painted. The paint is nearly worn off it. Will asks if this lamb came from the church box. Inside Bess's package is a cloth doll with a button missing from the doll's dress. Bess fingers the place where the button ought to be. Franco is watching me as I watch these youngsters open toys that were once hers. She sees my conflict and not theirs.

When we have wished everyone a Merry Christmas and said our good-byes and closed the front door, Franco asks me if I think the children liked my Christmas presents. I haven't got the heart to tell her, *About as much as you liked your hand-me-downs.* Instead I say, "It's a good thing I didn't see them first."

I put the screen in front of the fireplace and turn off the lights, and Franco and I start upstairs.

Halfway up we stop to rest. Franco tells me she is feeling pretty bad. I don't remember her ever admitting to such a thing. We sit together on the step in the dark and talk.

"When did you first know you were a lesbian?" Franco asks me.

"I don't know exactly. I was young."

"How did you know?"

"I went to the movies and stared at the women. I had crushes on my women teachers."

"But that's normal."

"Of course it's normal."

"I meant everyone has crushes."

"Somehow I knew mine were different. More serious, perhaps."

"Did you know any lesbians?"

"Not when I was young. I'd never even heard the word *lesbian*. Remember I grew up in Michigan, not New York."

"You must have seen masculine women. They have those in Michigan, don't they?"

"Sure. But I didn't identify with them any more than I identified with my girlfriends who were boy crazy. Those women looked like the boys I wasn't interested in. I wanted to be Grace Kelly and fall in love with her."

"When did you first kiss a woman passionately?"

"Not until you, Franco."

"Did you know I was a lesbian when you met me?"

"You know all this."

"How did you know I was?"

"By the way you looked at me in Duffy's. Are we going to stay here all night and talk?"

"Do you think you could carry me?"

"I could try."

"I don't think I can make it on my own."

Franco puts an arm around my shoulder, and I put an arm around her waist and lift her as best I can. We hobble to Franco's bedroom, and she sits on the edge of her bed while I undress her.

"By the time you got to college, did you know any lesbians?"

"Just in books. What's with all the questions, Franco?"

"I don't remember us ever talking about these things."

"Of course we did."

"I don't remember your answers. What about the books you read?"

"They were disappointing. They never had happy endings. One of the women always died or was redeemed by a man. Would you like me to rub your leg?"

"Yes, maybe that would help."

I go to the bathroom and return with the oil. We don't talk while I rub Franco's arms and legs. When I finish I pull the bed sheet and the comforter up over Franco and tell her, "I'm going to sleep in my room tonight so you can get a good night's

sleep." I turn off the light, and Franco whispers my name.
"Yes?"
"You're going to kiss me, aren't you?"
I lean down and kiss Franco good-night.
"I wish I didn't have to die so we could have a happy ending."
"Me, too, Franco."

Tuesday, December 24
Christmas Eve

I wake hoping it will be a good day for travel, but determined that no matter what kind of day it is, I will not give in and stay put.

In Franco's office, I make one call after another, crossing names off my list when the answer is no, and going on to the next. I have made two dozen calls before I get lucky and before Franco comes down to ask what I am up to.

"We're going to an inn," I answer, taking my glasses off to glance up at Franco who is standing in the doorway, blocking the sunlight that was streaking in from the kitchen.

"We're going where?"

"To an inn in Cazenovia," I answer.

"When?"

"As soon as you get dressed," I answer.

"I don't want to go anywhere, Thad."

"Well, we're going," I say.

"But I said I don't want to."

"I know you *said* that, but we're going. Come on, let's go up-stairs and pack."

"Thad!" Franco shouts, as I leave the room and her behind.

"What is it, Franco?"

"I'm not up to it."

I pay no attention to that remark and continue on my way, from the kitchen to the living room and on upstairs.

I have made my bed and hers by the time she comes into her room. "What do you want to wear?" I ask her.

"I'm not going anywhere, Thad. I want to stay here, in my home. You shouldn't have made my bed because I'm getting back into it."

"No, you're not," I say. "You're coming with me if I have to dress you and carry you."

"Why are you doing this?"

"How about your grey slacks and green sweater?" I ask, going to her wardrobe.

"Stop it!" she shouts.

"No, I won't. You invited me here to spend some time alone with you, and since we don't seem to be able to do that here, we're going away."

"What about Cleo?" Franco asks after a long pause. I know this is a last-ditch effort of hers to discourage me and that I've already won. Damn, why didn't I do this twenty years ago?

"She can take care of herself for one day. I could only get reservations for tonight. Now, do you want to wear your grey slacks and green sweater?"

Franco slumps down on her bed.

I go to my room, get my suitcase, and return to Franco. I set the suitcase on Franco's bed and open it. The items I'm taking are already packed in one side of it. I stand Franco up and take her robe off her. She remains standing.

"You can sit," I say. "I don't want your pajamas." I fold her robe and put it in the suitcase, go to her dresser and take out two pairs of socks and two sets of underwear. "Do you want me to pack a clean shirt for you to wear tomorrow? I've got one packed for me."

Franco nods her head.

I go to the bathroom and fill the tub and call to Franco. She comes in, still looking overwhelmed. "Take off your pajamas and get in," I say.

"If you minded yesterday so much, why didn't you say so?"

"I didn't mind it so much. Get in the tub."

"Then why are you doing this?"

I help Franco into the tub.

"Franco, we are running out of time, and I'm not going to spend the next thirty years without you wishing I'd done this."

Franco looks astonished that I would be so blunt. It's true it has been more her style than mine. "I've taken a page out of your book," I admit.

"I'm glad you've learned something," Franco says in mock disgust as I get up from the commode to leave her be while she bathes. And with a shrug I let her know I agree with her estimation of me.

Too soon cute and too late smart, I think, as I snap our suitcase shut in the next room. Who said that? My grandmother did. It was one of her standard remarks to Wesley and me during our teen-age years.

By noon, Franco and I are on the road. We couldn't ask for a better day. The sky is cloudless and the roads are dry, and once we are beyond Ostego Lake there is no traffic. The country-side is rolling farmland, dairy mostly, and there are cows grazing on bundles of hay in the snow-covered meadows. Some part of me, the dreamer in me, wants to drive on, not stop when we reach Cazenovia. I never imagined Franco coming out to California to live with me. I always pictured me returning to her, but now I want to leave the East and our past behind us and continue westward. Into the sunset, I guess.

"It's Christmas Eve," Franco says out of the blue. We haven't spoken for many miles.

I'm expecting something more so I say, "Yes?"

Franco looks at me and says, "Tomorrow is Christmas and you're here."

"And?"

"And I didn't know if I would be able to get you here," she says. "I worried for days. I even spoke to Nell."

"And what did Nell say?" I ask.

"She didn't understand why I had trouble asking you to come. But I had to ask you in a way that you would for sure come, and I didn't want to tell you I was sick."

"Why is that?"

"I didn't want you to come out of pity. I didn't want this to be a mercy mission."

"But you did tell me."

"I waited so long to ask you that I had to tell you."

"Well, it wasn't a pitiful letter, and you aren't pitiful, and I don't pity you."

"I'm so glad. I can't tell you."

"It was really that hard? I wouldn't have believed it. Your letter sounded almost casual . . . straightforward and composed."

"If you didn't come, I was going to go to you."

I reach beside me for Franco's hand.

The Lakeside Inn is on Cazenovia Lake. It is a white clapboard house with green window trim and no shutters. It has a plain and friendly look the way a girl's camp does. It isn't posh like so many inns are these days. On the back, which is actually the front, there is a long porch overlooking the lake. It is not in use in the winter, but there is a dining room just inside the porch and from there we will look out on the frozen lake as we eat dinner.

Our room has its own sitting room and bath. It is the only suite at the Inn, and available because the folks who reserved it for this last week in December are a day late in arriving. A raft of old *Colliers* magazines are on the table in the sitting room, and Franco gets her nose into them the moment we arrive.

I unpack, take my clothes off, and get into bed. When Franco becomes aware that I've quieted down, she peeks her head around the corner and asks, "Are you sleeping or waiting for me?"

"If you don't hurry up," I say, "it will be the other."

She puts her magazine down.

I watch Franco take off her sweater, fold it, and set it on the dresser, then remove her slacks and lay them neatly over the chair. She stands before me in her underpants and socks. Franco doesn't need a bra; her breasts are small and firm. She bends down to take off her socks, then her underpants and is naked before me. I am hoping she won't come to bed just yet. Let me look at her, let me admire her flat stomach and firm thighs, let me imagine my hand along her side, touching the curve of her breast. Let me look at her until neither of us can stand it any longer, until we must touch to relieve our longing.

Franco gives me a smirk. It is as though she can read my mind and therefore my desire. Then she reaches down for the covering on the bed and pulls it back off me. And she slides into bed and on top of me. I can see only her face now, and that is out of focus. I close my eyes and feel her. I feel the weight of her, and the coolness of her, and the heartbeat of her. We kiss and then she slides down, away from my kiss, to make love to me.

I have a picture of her in my mind. She is sitting across from me in Duffy's. Her hair is mussed, her cheeks are rosy from the cold outdoors, her eyes are large and blue and open wide in a bold-faced expression. She has just asked me if I am glad I let her talk me into a sled ride. I can't say how glad I am but I know that the world has changed entirely for me. Sitting across from her at that table with the red formica top, I glance up into those intense eyes and fiddle with the corner of my paper napkin. I cannot believe what all my senses tell me, that this woman likes me.

Franco says my name, and the sound of her voice is intimate and reassuring. I open my eyes and look into hers. She tells me she loves me. She holds me in her arms, wrapping her legs around me as well, and we fall asleep. When we wake we talk to one another in whispers.

How do you feel?
You must be hungry.
Do you want to bathe first?
You are beautiful.
Let's stay here forever.
They'll kick us out.
We'll buy the place.
I'm getting hungry.
Was that your stomach?
You go first.
Do you really love me?
You don't mind that I'm spoiled goods?
I never knew you were a worrier.
God, I'm hungry.
Let's take one together.

Every table in the dining room is occupied. Dinner is being served at one time for all the Inn's guests—perhaps twenty. Red linen tablecloths and centerpieces of holly are on all the tables, and candles are glowing everywhere, on the mantle over the cobblestone fireplace, on each table, and in the windows. Without knowing any of the people who surround us, we nevertheless feel the warmth of familiarity. We are surrounded by and take for granted the kindness of friends we don't know. It is partly this perception which has made inns popular, I think.

I can't imagine Franco and me feeling better off at home, and she agrees with me. Once our dinner plates have been set down in front of us and the waitress has left, Franco says, "I'm glad we're here. I feel far away from everyone and everything."

The meal is not spectacular, but satisfactory and filling. Afterward, Franco and I put on our coats and go for a walk on the lake. It is as glorious a night as it was a glorious day. The sky is black and cloudless. The stars and three-quarter moon are up and bright. We walk quite a ways out on the lake, and from there the tiny lights strung around the porch and the candles in the windows look like a reflection of the stars overhead.

We can hear the notes of familiar Christmas carols being played on a piano at the inn.

We walk with our arms around one another, for warmth and in love, and talk about our last two visits, seven and five years ago.

"Why didn't you let me sleep with you when I came out to California?" Franco asks.

"You were leaving the next day," I answer.

"I asked you if you were involved and you didn't answer me. Were you?"

"I was," I say, "and if I'd slept with you and then you left, I couldn't go back to Carol."

"What happened to her?"

"I wasn't in love with her. What about you five years ago?"

"Your surprise visit?"

"Did I interrupt something?"

"As a matter of fact, I had plans the night you arrived."

"And what became of her?"

"She graduated."

"Then she was young," I say, surprised.

"No. She had returned to school after raising a family."

"She wasn't free then. She was married."

"She was free and wanted to stay that way."

"And that didn't suit you?"

Franco doesn't answer.

"You were in love," I say.

"I was infatuated," she answers.

"And when she left?"

"I felt badly for a couple months."

I think about whether I will respond honestly or not and decide to be honest. "Of course I'm jealous," I say, and Franco laughs. I ask her what's so funny about me being jealous, and she says, "That you would be jealous over something that happened five years ago."

"You're too sensible, Franco. You don't understand the irrational mind."

"And that's truly funny," she says.

"All right, cut it out."

"I think the joke's on me, Thad, because you need your jealousy to make yourself feel lucky to have me."

"No, I don't."

"Don't answer so fast. Think about it."

"I don't need to think about it," I say.

"That sounds like, 'I don't want to think about it.' "

"Franco, are we going to fight on Christmas Eve?"

"Are you going to ever believe that I love you?" she asks.

We change the subject, or I do, but later when we have returned to our room, Franco says, "You could make the choice to. What harm could it do you?"

I know what she is referring to without her telling me because her question was left hanging in mid-air.

When we returned to our room we found a stocking hanging on our door and every door down the hall. Beyond it our bed has been tidied and two candy canes placed on the pillows.

"Do you ever wonder what people think when two women our age take a room with a double bed?"

"I think they think we're sleeping together," Franco answers matter-of-factly.

"Do they talk among themselves about us, do you think?"

"Are you worried or does it excite you to imagine they do?"

"There is a certain thrill to illicitness."

Franco sits down on the bed to rest before undressing. She was the one to suggest a walk, and she has paid a high price. "I suppose," she says, "when we're out of the closet completely, some of us won't like being acceptable."

I undress and put on my robe, then turn to Franco. "What is it?" I ask, but I can see she is having trouble breathing and I go to her. "I'm not listening to you anymore," I say, and I put my hand on her abdomen. "Come on," I say, coaxing her to take a deep breath. "Lie back, then. It might be easier." Franco looks panicky. "Imagine yourself breathing easily," I say. "That's it. You see you can."

I help Franco undress, then sit cross-legged at the foot of the bed and massage her feet while I sing to her. It's a song I sang to Wesley when he was scared, and it does the trick. Franco falls fast asleep. I don't get into bed with her immediately. For a while I sit up in the chair and watch her sleep.

After a moment I ask myself why we are here. What did I hope to find here? Do here? Recapture here? Or get away from here? Are you running out to your tree as you did when you were a child? But running, this time, with someone. I remember the first line of a healing poem which goes: *While you were sleeping, all the cupboards of the earth were filled*. But I can't remember the rest, only a vague idea of what follows, which I keep confusing with the Mother Hubbard poem. I am frustrated because I cannot remember the poem, and afraid that because I can't, Franco can't be healed. Then, suddenly, I feel angry at her for being sick, for getting sick, for not making herself well now that she is sick, and I go get a magazine and return to the chair with the hope of getting my mind off all this.

But it's no use. I can't read the magazine. I probably don't want to be distracted. After all, I didn't run to my tree to get away from pain. I ran there to feel my pain in private—to allow it, not repress it. Then why can't I cry? Am I being stubborn? Is it that I have not accepted that Franco won't get well? Maybe that's why I can't cry. But I have cried. Just now I can't. And why is that? Is it because we don't make steady progress? We go forward and fall back and go forward and fall back? Could it be we don't get over our anger and self-pity and move on to mourning, or whatever the so-called stages are, but rather we get over our anger and self-pity, then suddenly we are back with them again. Maybe there isn't a neat order to things. Isn't Franco sad and happy, relieved and worried, angry and forgiving? Just as I am.

I want to give up this notion of "overcoming." I want to be able to accept retreat, even withdrawal. I want to be able to accept her withdrawal. I don't want to fight so much. I want to be able to look at her losing things and not feel I must, for her sake and mine, step in, interrupt her progress in that. Yes, I could see it as progress, couldn't I? Do I know it is not progress? That night I prayed that God would heal Franco through me and was told something better was at work. . .could I. . .is it within my abilities to believe that is true? What if I could believe she loves me and that what is happening to her is not bad?

As I wonder about this, something wonderful happens to me. I am filled with joy, or emptied of despair, and I know this feeling. It is the feeling I had when, finally, it dawned on me, or sunk in, that three times zero was not three but zero. I had fought that one hard, unwilling to accept what I was told and what others believed. Maybe not wanting to. Maybe feeling threatened and thinking that to stay alive, to keep from being swallowed up, I had to stick stubbornly to my beliefs.

You do not have to be afraid comes through. I don't know who says this to me, but I marvel at the message, so clear and believable, and I turn off the light and get into bed.

Wednesday, December 25
Christmas Day

I open my eyes and see Franco sitting up in bed, looking through one of the *Colliers* magazines. The others are stacked on the table beside her. She isn't aware I'm awake. I watch her turn a page. She has such thin wrists and long, elegant fingers. Beautiful hands.

"Merry Christmas," I say.

"Good morning. I've been waiting for you."

"With your nose in a magazine."

"These are wonderful."

"And why is that?" I ask, getting up to go to the bathroom. I can hear her answer from the next room.

"They're so cheerful and optimistic. Not like today's magazines which are full of bad news and criticism. Have you noticed, even the ads these days have negative connotations?"

"No," I say, returning to the bedroom. "Lately it's seemed to me that Pollyanna was making a comeback."

"Do you want some coffee?"

"Where'd you get that?" I ask, noticing the tray from room service.

"I called for it this morning."

"I must have been sleeping soundly," I say, putting my robe on.

Before I can sit down on the bed, Franco says, "Go get our stocking off the door."

"Have you been up all night listening for Santa Claus?" I go to the door, listen for quiet in the hall, then open our door and take the stocking from it.

Franco puts her magazine aside, and I give her the stocking to empty. In it are a small bag of nuts, another of candy, a Christmas card with a photograph of the Lakeside Inn in winter and an invitation to a complimentary breakfast, a pen with a Santa and "Lakeside Inn" printed on it, a sachet of honeysuckle, and a bar of pine-scented soap. "I would like the soap," Franco says. "You can have the pen and sachet. We'll put the card on the mantle at home and eat the nuts and candy."

"That takes care of that," I say. "I guess you're ready for breakfast now?"

"Not yet," Franco says. She puts everything back in the stocking and reaches forward to open my robe. I move away, and she asks, "Why did you do that?"

"I'm tired," I say.

"It's Christmas, Thad. You're not going to sleep in on Christmas, are you?"

"Where's that coffee you offered me?"

Franco pours me a cup and asks, "Don't you want to?"

"You're in rare form today," I say. "How long have you been up anyway?"

"For a while. I had a bad dream and couldn't go back to sleep."

"What about?" I ask, taking a sip of coffee. "Shit! This stuff isn't even warm."

"I dreamed a big black and white cat came into our yard. Really big, the size of a person. And Cleo tried to scare it away, but it wasn't the least bit scared of her. It raised its paw and swatted at her and caught her in its claws. It was going to kill her, so I ran out. I was scared of the cat, too, but I knew it would kill Cleo if I didn't stop it. I pretended I was fierce. I made a horrible face and screamed and waved my arms in the air and it ran off. Then I went to Cleo and saw she had these tiny puncture holes all over her body where droplets of blood were oozing out. I licked at them but they wouldn't stop bleeding, and I knew if I didn't think of something, Cleo would bleed to death."

"Did you think of something?"

"No, I woke up. And then I couldn't get back to sleep. I was worried something had really happened to Cleo and here I was unable to help her."

"Nothing's happened to Cleo."

"You don't know that."

"It was a dream about you, not Cleo."

Franco looks at me with that intense stare she gets when she is thinking hard about something. "It might have been about me," she says after a moment.

I take off my robe and get under the covers with her. For all her eagerness, Franco proceeds slowly in lovemaking. She eats fast, talks fast, thinks fast, and used to move fast, but when being made love to, she slows herself down and holds herself back. The morning is not my best time. It takes me a while to rally. I fade in and out, can't hold my concentration, and I'm tempted to drift back to sleep when being made love to. Franco *is* a morning person, and more than that, her sense of aliveness is closely linked to sexual expression. Whenever she has felt least alive, she has wanted most to make love. The opposite is true for me. Naturally.

After our lovemaking, Franco bathes and I pack us up. Then I bathe. It takes her twice as long to dress these days, so we finish at about the same time.

Franco glances back at the room as we step out.

"They'd probably sell you a magazine if you asked," I say.

"Nah."

"If it makes you feel good."

"Nah, it belongs here. Let's go."

We are shown to the same table in the dining room we ate

at the night before. Today the sun is so bright coming in the lakeside windows that the shades are pulled down halfway. Franco asks that ours be pulled up so that we can enjoy the sun on us.

It is easy to picture this place on a summer day when the lake is blue and flowing. I would like to return here then. Allowing this thought to take the shape of words in my mind has a consequence. Franco asks me what's wrong, and I say, "The sun is very bright."

She studies me.

"I'm O.K.," I say. "I shouldn't have looked directly into it."

"It isn't the sun, is it?" she asks, and I just smile. "You never sang to me before last night," Franco says, changing the subject for both our sakes. "I wonder if there's something I've never done for you."

"I've heard you sing," I say.

"There must be something. I'm going to think of it. It will be my Christmas present to you."

After breakfast we drive to town, park the car at the small public park by the lake, and get out. We stand for minutes and look out in silence, then Franco says, "Let's go home, Thad." Her tone has changed from lightheartedness to resignation.

We return to the car.

We do not talk much in the car on the trip home. It doesn't feel like Christmas. Except that this is how Christmas has often felt to me. The elaborate preparations and expectations for Christmas make the day itself a disappointment. I feel let down.

"What time is it?" Franco asks when we are about an hour from Woodbine.

"It gets dark early, doesn't it?"

"I hate arriving home when it's dark, and there aren't any lights on in the house. I wish I'd left a light on. Poor Cleo, in the dark, wondering where we are and if we'll ever return."

"Franco, do you remember the debate on Willis Street over using animals in medical research?"

"It sounds familiar," she says.

"You and I were on opposite sides until you did an about-face. When I thanked you for coming to my rescue, you said that wasn't what you'd done."

"And you're still mad about that?"

"No, I never believed you. Wasn't it that you didn't want me to think you'd rescued me?"

"I don't remember."

"Come on, I'm not eighteen, I know when you're sidestepping. I'm not letting you off the hook, Franco. I want an answer."

"Why?"

"Because I do."

"I suppose I didn't want you to expect me to rescue you, as you put it. Especially not from a situation where you could rescue yourself. Women do that too much and don't ever get to know their own strengths. But I'm sure I must have agreed with your argument because I wouldn't have agreed just for the sake of helping you out. I wouldn't do that."

"No kidding!"

"Satisfied?"

"Yes."

"Tying up loose ends, Thad?"

Of course I am and wish she didn't always understand my motives. It makes it impossible for me to pretend we aren't concluding something. I feel guilty for wanting to set things straight, for needing to, for that being foremost on my mind when the more important concern ought to be that she is dying. But if I try to explain to Franco that losing her means I am running out of time to ask her things I need to know, I will sound so selfish. *Too bad you're dying, kid. But before you pop off, I need to know a few things.*

When we arrive home, Franco stays in the car while I run in the house to turn on the Christmas tree lights. Then I return to the car for Franco and our suitcase. Franco's head is bowed. This gives me a sudden start. During the last hour all I've thought about is her dying, and suddenly it looks as if she has.

"Franco!" I cry, sounding desperate.

She lifts her head, and I see tears. I reach my hand in the car and touch the top of her head. She puts her hand on mine and gives it a squeeze. I take my hand away and run around to the other side of the car, get in, and hold her in my arms. She cries softly, then laughs. Is she losing her mind? I wonder.

"Why did you laugh just then?" I ask.

"I suddenly saw how ridiculous we are."

"We aren't ridiculous," I argue.

"Well, yes, in a way we are, Thad. Let's go in."

Franco and I sit on the floor in front of a fire—Cleo on Franco's lap—and eat sandwiches I've made from the leftover turkey. We don't talk at all. I don't want to tell Franco what's on my mind, and I don't want to know what's on hers. I'm shut down. I'm depressed by us, depressed that Christmas is over, depressed that I can't look forward to anything good happening. I'm ready to cash in my chips. Why the hell not? I hate this damn life. Just when things are looking up, something comes along to spoil everything. I want to kick that damn Christmas tree over, set this house on fire. Kill or be killed, that's how I feel. I can't sit here any longer. The pain is excruciating. I get up off the floor, run upstairs, and throw myself on my bed. But I don't cry. I can't let go of my rage to cry. Minutes pass.

Then, "I love you," Franco says softly. I roll over and I can see her silhouette in the open doorway.

"I don't want to hear that!" I shout at her. I'm shocked by my gruffness. But I don't stop there. "I don't want you to love me," I say. "I hate me and I hate you! I hate it all!"

"No, you don't," she says. "You love it all or you wouldn't be in this predicament."

Franco comes over to me, turns on the low light beside the bed, and sits down on the bed. She tries to stroke my head, but I push her hand away.

"Don't do that," she says firmly.

"I told you I don't want you to love me. Get away from me."

Instead of doing as I say, Franco gets up on the bed and takes me in her arms. "My death will be too hard on you if you don't listen to me."

"About what?" I ask, still sounding angry.

"Let up on yourself, Thad. And on me."

"Explain that, please."

"You can't possibly understand it all. And you don't have to. Don't expect yourself to. You hurt and so you say you hate it all. Some part of you wants to hate because you think it would hurt less if you did. It wouldn't. Thad, I love you because you feel deeply about things and express how you feel, because you are not indifferent or hateful. You love life and yourself, and I know you love me. If you try to kid yourself about that, or try to kill that in you, you're sunk."

"I don't want you to die," I say.

"No, but between now and then you'll come to accept it, I'm sure."

"I won't."

"Yes, you will."

"Do you?"

"I will," she says.

We are quiet for a moment. Then Franco says, "Let's go down, it's cold up here."

On our way downstairs we hear something and go to the front window to look out. Coming up the walk are five carolers with candles. Franco and I put on our coats, stand in the open doorway, and are serenaded. When the singing stops, one of the carolers steps forward and she and Franco hug.

Franco introduces me to her and then to the others. "This is my friend, Thaddea Owens." I don't remember hearing Franco say my full name before and I swell with pride hearing her voice say it.

The five carolers wish us a Merry Christmas and start away. One of them waves at the end of the walkway and calls back, "Good-night, Doctor Cole." How can she quit teaching? I wonder. I would work up to the last minute to have those young loyalists around me.

Franco and I return to the floor in front of the warm fire. I feel Franco watching me too closely, and it makes me uneasy. I am breaking down and I don't want even her to see me do that. I try to ignore her, but in avoiding her something equally unpleasant comes to my mind.

One year on Christmas Eve my father came home from an office party stinking drunk. Well, not one year, every year, but this one he forgot he was supposed to pick up a tree on his way home. He and Mother had one of their arguments that turned into a brawl, and Wesley and I ran and hid in the closet in my room. When things calmed down downstairs, Mother came and got Wesley and me and took us downstairs. I was sure Father had ordered her to bring us to him. Not to apologize to us but to defend himself. I remember I was no longer scared. I thought, I'm going to tell him he is a bad man. Father wasn't there waiting for Wesley and me. He wasn't even in the house. Two shopping bags were standing in the middle of the living room. Wesley and my Christmas presents were in them. They were not wrapped. Mother hadn't gotten around to wrapping them yet. She gave one bag to me and one to Wesley and said good-night. Wesley and I were quite confused. Were we supposed to look inside the bags?

We knew what the next day, Christmas Day, would be like. Mother and Father would be sick, and Wesley and I would be alone to do whatever we wanted. No, not whatever we wanted, because what we wanted was to do something, anything, as a family.

Wesley always blamed himself for Mother and Father's difficulties. I was younger than he, but I knew that he had nothing to do with the way they were and I told him so. He didn't trust me. He hated himself too much. I hated them. Wesley thought he was bad. I felt he was very wrong, but not bad.

I realize now that he felt he was bad because he was so badly treated. And Vietnam clinched the deal for Wesley. Once you accept a wrong idea it's hard as hell to get rid of it. Everything seems to prove its validity.

One day, Wesley and a Vietnamese kid were face to face, grenade to gun, and Wesley threw his grenade and blew the kid to smithereens. Then five years later he shot himself to even the score.

"I'd like to talk," Franco says, bringing me back to her.

"I'm too tired," I say, assuming she means that she wants me to talk to her.

"I'll tell you whatever you want to know. You ask and I'll answer."

"This isn't you talking," I say, a bit sarcastic.

"I know I've been stingy in that way, but lately I've made an effort."

"Do you think maybe you're losing your mind?"

"Is that a serious question for me to answer, or are you joking?"

"Joking. But I do have a serious question. Are you afraid of dying?"

"Yes, I'm afraid of dying. But not death."

"What about it?"

"I'm afraid of becoming helpless, of not being able to take care of myself. Of becoming pathetic and ugly. I don't want to look in the mirror and be revolted by what I see."

I don't dare tell Franco that before seeing her looking so well, I was afraid of that.

"Have you seen anyone in the last stages of ALS?"

"I saw someone on TV, and Jacob Javits."

"How did they look to you?"

"Pretty bad."

"Yep."

"But you're not afraid of death itself?"

"No."

"What do you think happens?"

"I don't know. I hope it's not a big nothing."

"If you don't know, how come you're not afraid?"

"I don't know that either."

"Why did you cry in the car earlier?"

"Thad, I don't know that either. I promise I'm not avoiding answering you. I don't have the answers to those questions. I cried in the car because I couldn't not cry. That maybe doesn't make sense. I can't make sense of it. It wasn't seeing the tree lights, if that's what you think, or coming back here."

"I understand," I say. "It happens to me."

"Anything else you'd like to ask me?"

"Not tonight," I say. "Does this privilege extend to tomorrow?" Franco nods her head.

"I'm too tired to go on. Let's go to bed. To sleep," I add.

"Can I ask you something?"

"Yes."

"Those years we took turns spending weekends in Baltimore and New York, did you stop enjoying sex with me for some reason you could tell me?"

"Because I just said that about going to bed to sleep?"

"That brought it back to mind."

"You seemed only interested in me in that way, and I wanted more. I wanted emotional intimacy."

"I thought that might be it."

"Then or now?" I ask.

"Now. Then, too, perhaps. I knew you were mad at me. You were always a little mad at me because you weren't getting what you wanted from me. I didn't ask you what that was because I didn't want to get into it with you. So I must have known you wanted more emotional support. I settled for less than I wanted to avoid giving more than I wanted."

I stand and put the screen in front of the fireplace. Franco also stands.

"What have you got on your head?" she asks me.

I raise my hand to my head. "Nothing," I say.

"Yes, you do," Franco insists. She reaches up and brings down an old 3 x 5 snapshot of me.

"Where'd you get that?" I ask, astonished.

She shrugs her shoulders and puts her hands in her pockets. "What's in your pockets?"

Franco takes her hands out, then pulls a coin out from behind my right ear and another from behind my left.

"Merry Christmas, Thad." She places both coins in my hand.

"When did you learn magic?" I ask her.

"I taught myself when I was a kid," she answers, smiling brightly. "Still pretty good, too. I fooled you."

We turn off the tree lights and the house lights and go up to bed.

Thursday, December 26
Woodbine

I roll over in bed and realize I am alone in it. Where am I? Am I back in San Francisco? What happened to our last day together? I hear the toilet flush and open my eyes. Music never sounded better to me. A moment later Franco steps into the room.

"What are you thinking?" she asks me.

"Nothing. Just looking for you."

"That's a very wistful expression you're wearing. Does the sight of me make you wistful?"

Of course it does, but I lie and say no.

"Good. Then why *are* you wistful?"

Why are you pushing this? I wonder. "I was remembering how the shadow of Bradley Hall would move up Smith Hall as the sun was setting." Franco asks me to explain this. "During English classes I used to look out the window and watch the shadow of Bradley Hall, where I was, move up the side of the building across from it. Are you getting back in bed?" I ask.

"What did you have in mind?" Franco asks.

"Well, you do look pretty cute standing there."

Franco is standing naked as the day she was born at the foot of her bed.

"Aren't you cold?" I ask.

"Is that an invitation?"

"Yes."

Franco climbs back into bed and asks me, "Don't you have a Christmas present for me?"

"My God, Franco, I forgot it!" I crawl out of bed, go across the hall, and return with her gift.

When we get up, sometime later, Franco says she wants to hang the bird feeder and then take a walk on campus and go to Duffy's for lunch. After breakfast we hang the feeder.

I carry the ladder from the shed to the back of the house, and Franco climbs up it. I have always been afraid of ladders.

"Are you sure about this?" I ask her, as she starts up with a hammer sticking out of her back pocket and the bird feeder in one hand. I can't look up at her as she climbs because it would be impossible not to imagine myself doing it.

"Be quiet!" she hollers down to me. "I need to concentrate."

"If you think it's more than you can do, don't do it," I say, standing with my head bowed, supporting the legs of the ladder which are well enough supported by the foot of snow they are sunk into.

Franco nails the feeder into the corner post of her house, where cats and squirrels have no chance of getting at the birds who come to the feeder.

"How long do you think before they'll discover it?" Franco asks, once she is back on the ground.

"If they're hungry, not long. They'll check it out for a day or two to be certain it's safe."

"What will I do about refilling it when they've eaten all the seeds?"

I start to say, "You just refill it," when I realize the dilemma. "Oh, shit, Franco. What a couple of dummies we are."

"I'd have to get the ladder out every time, wouldn't I?"

"Well, you can't do that."

We decide we must move the feeder to a better place, below the bathroom window. When that is done, Franco rests on the rock by the pump while I put the ladder away in the shed. When I return to her I notice a glazed expression on her face.

"Shall we go?" I ask.

"I wasn't sure I could tell you I was sick," Franco says, looking miles away. Then her eyes blink, and she stops staring off and squints at me. "You would want to know everything. Your need to know everything has always scared me. If you did come, I knew I would have to give you what you wanted or you would leave. I'd have to talk, tell you things."

"I don't think I would have," I say. "I might have wanted to leave, but I wouldn't have been able to."

"I never withheld from you to be mean, you know?"

"I do now."

"I was afraid of you, Thad."

"What about me?" I ask. "That I was in love with you?"

"No, I wanted you to be in love with me. But when you started talking about your feelings I felt you wanted me to also."

"I did."

"I didn't want to talk about feelings."

"Why?"

"I was afraid I might give in to them."

"Not talking about them, you gave in to fear."

"I think so, Thad. Let's go in. I want to call Peg."

While Franco calls Peg from her office, I go into the living room to read. Then I remember all those bluebooks I packed and haven't bothered to look at, and I go upstairs to get them.

A couple hours pass before I put the last of the books down and look up at the clock surprised. I had expected Franco to interrupt me. I listen for her now but the house is still, and I get up from the couch and take the stack of bluebooks upstairs with me to look in on her. Franco is not upstairs, nor downstairs, and I begin to worry where she might be when I glimpse her out the kitchen window, sitting on the rock by the pump.

I open the back door and a flight of sparrows sails across the yard to a maple tree.

"They've discovered it already," Franco sings out. "It's great!"

"I'm sorry I scared them off," I say, and she motions for me to come out. I go get my coat.

"I hope that doesn't mean they've been starving," Franco says when I join her in the backyard.

"What about you? Aren't you starving?"

"Did you finish grading your papers?" Franco asks.

"Yes, why didn't you interrupt me? I was only doing it while you talked to Peg. How is Peg?"

"She's O.K."

"How was it talking to her?"

"It was O.K."

" 'It was O.K.' doesn't tell me much, Franco."

"It was hard at first. She was embarrassed about the other day, about us seeing her that way. She asked me what you thought."

"And what did you tell her?"

"I told her your parents were alcoholics. She's sober again, and she says this time it's for good."

"Did you tell her about you?"

"No. I thought about it, but she sounded so up. I didn't want to give her anything to get down about."

Franco takes one of my hands in hers and holds it tightly. Then she looks up at me the way you might if you thought what you were looking at might vanish any second. It is a desperate look. I give her a moment and then I say, "What is it, Franco?"

"What time do you leave tomorrow?" she asks.

I can't answer her.

"What time is your flight?" she asks.

"I'll go fix us lunch," I say, and I jump up from the rock and hurry inside.

In the kitchen darkness closes in around me. At first, it's just my peripheral vision, then everything goes black. Then I feel a hand on my shoulder and I hear Franco's voice say, "Thad?"

I look up and Franco is standing before me in her peacoat. I am sitting on a kitchen chair.

"Are you all right?" she asks.

I shake my head. "Everything went blank, Franco. I panicked and a curtain pulled closed."

"You're flushed," she says, and she puts her cool hands on my cheeks.

"I'm all right. I'm better now."

Franco makes us sandwiches for lunch, and we go into the living room to eat them. She puts a record album on and we sit together on the couch.

"After lunch we'll get out, we'll go for a walk," she says. "We'll still go to Duffy's, but we'll have a soda instead of lunch."

"I don't want to go there," I say, and I stand up. Leaving my lunch untouched on the coffee table, I retreat upstairs.

Franco comes into the guest room where I am, undresses herself, then comes over to me and starts to undress me.

"What are you doing?" I ask her, but she doesn't answer me.

We get into bed. We don't make love. We lie together, holding on to one another in silence. After a while I begin to feel stronger. I'm not leaving, I tell myself. No matter what Franco says or does, I'm staying. I know she wants me to stay. She just can't say it. I'll call Martha and tell her to take Edna home with her or put her on a plane and send her to me.

"You mean more to me than anyone," Franco says in a whisper.

"Not more than your family," I answer.

"Yes, more than anyone," she says, but is quick to add, "except me."

"You would add that," I say.

"I would," she says with a smile.

"I could kill you, Franco."

"That won't be necessary."

"Oh, Franco..."

"Oh, come on, Thad, this isn't the end of everything. For all you know it could mark the beginning of something for you."

"Don't say crap like that! I know what this is."

"Boy, you are stubborn with your pain."

"What the hell does that mean?"

"It means you enjoy it."

I pull away from Franco and get out of bed. "Damn you," I say. "Do you honestly think I enjoy this? Do you? Do you think this is *fun* for me? I wish I'd never come. Goddamnit! I wish I'd never fallen in love with you in the first place." Franco sits up in bed and I gulp air. I hate these words. Why am I saying them?

"It's all right," Franco says calmly.

"It's not all right," I say, turning away in shame.

"Thad, you're going to be all right because you *never could* count on me."

"Oh, Franco. . .why?"

Franco gets out of bed, comes over to me, and puts her arms around me. "I'm sorry, Thad. I'm truly sorry. I know this has been difficult for you. I guess it was unrealistic and selfish of me to invite you here. Will you ever forgive me?"

I start to cry and can't talk. We sit down on the bed together. Franco takes my hand and strokes it with one of hers. "I should have done better than this," I apologize. "I didn't want to be like this. I wanted to be strong. Oh, God, I wanted so to be strong for you."

"You're only human, Thad. And you've been wonderful. What the hell did we expect, that this would be easy?"

"Oh, God, I love you so, Franco. I love you so. I don't want to go tomorrow. I don't want to lose you. Won't you please get better. Please, for me?"

Tears are streaming down Franco's cheeks, and she is smiling at me.

We get back into bed, and this time we fall asleep and don't wake until it is dark out. Cleo wakes us. She jumps up on the bed and lets out a nasty meow to let us know she is hungry.

"What time is it?" Franco asks.

I can't read the clock because it is too dark in the room. I have a terrible sinking feeling in my stomach. It's gone; the day is gone, our last day together.

"Too late for a walk, now," Franco says. "Ah, well, it's just as well."

We put on our robes and go downstairs. I put the turkey in the oven to warm, and the smell of it makes me squeamish. I know I'm not going to be able to eat it, so I open a can of soup for me, and a half hour later, Franco and I are sitting across from one another at the dining room table. Franco looks old to me, much older than she looked the evening I arrived.

"I can't do it, Franco."

"Do what?" she asks. I put down my spoon and she says, "Eat?"

"No, I can't leave you tomorrow."

"You have to, Thad."

I shake my head and Franco looks down. She is quiet for so long I think maybe she is going to give in to me, but when she lifts her head she says, "If I were you I'd leave. I'd love you, but I'd leave you."

"You're not me," I say.

"I want you to leave me, Thad. I look at you and I see what I am losing—what I will lose. I wouldn't be able to stand it, Thad. Don't you see it would be too painful? Do you want to torture me?"

I can't answer her because to answer no would be to give in to her.

"All our sweetness would turn to despair. I don't want that, Thad."

"This is despair," I argue.

"Yes."

No, that's not my argument. "Being apart would be despair," I say.

"You can't stay," Franco answers flatly. "You must leave for both our sakes."

"Not my sake."

"Yes, yours, too. If you interrupt your life, it'll be even harder for you to return to it when I die. If you give up your friends and your job out there and lose me, where will you be?"

"No worse off than I am now."

"Yes, much worse."

"Franco, I feel married to you. I don't want to leave you no matter what the consequences might be." Please, Franco, I plead as I wait for her response.

"I can't give you anything more, Thad."

Franco's words cut into me so horribly, I can't look at her after she's said them. I get up from the table and go upstairs to pack. As I fold my clothes and put them into my suitcase, I feel as if pieces of my flesh are being torn away. Franco comes into the room while I am finishing packing and asks me to come to her room when I am done.

She is sitting in one of the chairs by the fireplace with Cleo on her lap when I step into her room. She asks me to sit in the other chair, and I do.

"I want you to come back and help me die," she says. "Would you do that? And take Cleo? Would you take Cleo?"

"Now?"

"No, later."

I nod my head as I stare at the flames of the fire.

"Oh, thank God," she says with relief, and I turn and look at her. "I've been worried about Cleo."

"I don't understand you, Franco. Don't you know I'd do anything you asked?"

"But you have Edna."

"Why don't you take me for granted? I wanted to be taken for granted, Franco."

"I'm not going to hang on for dear life when it's no longer a dear life. Do you understand?"

I nod my head.

"You won't fight me on this?"

"I won't," I say.

"I haven't decided what I'm going to do. I'd like to just will myself to die."

"How like you," I say, forced to smile.

"I'll work it out and make sure you're free of any possible blame. I don't think I should tell you."

"I understand," I say.

"I've got a notebook with everything in it. Everything you'll need to know. Names and addresses of people. Things I want friends and family to have, that kind of stuff. Will you take care of that for me?"

"I will," I say. I don't know which one of us has backed away, but we seem to be talking to one another across a great distance.

"I don't want a ceremony," Franco says, "and I'd like to be cremated. You can decide what to do with my ashes."

"How soon?" I ask.

"As soon as I can no longer take care of myself."

"How soon will that be?"

"Six months."

Six months, I repeat to myself. Six months. I could get a leave of absence for six months. "What about in the meantime?" I ask. "Who's going to rub your arms and legs when you get a cramp? What if you fall or get into some kind of trouble?"

"Nell is going to be coming by."

"You've already arranged that?" I ask, feeling betrayed by both of them. I look at Franco. She nods her head. "I don't want her here instead of me," I say. "I don't want her rubbing your legs."

"I'm not doing this to hurt you, Thad."

"I'm going to hate the world when you're no longer in it."

"I don't think so."

"You don't know me without you."

"No, we never know that, do we."

Franco gets up and goes to her bed. I stay put as long as I can. I want her to wonder if I will come to her. I want her to worry that I might not. The fire is the only light in the room.

Franco sits up in bed, leaning back against the headboard, looking in my direction. I cannot see her eyes. I hope they are open.

"You have a good chunk of life ahead of you," she says. "I
know you will be happy. I know you will love and be loved."

Why does she insist upon that?

"I have something for you that I don't want you to take liter-
ally." Franco removes a ring from her hand. "I don't want you
tied to the memory of me, Thad. This is a symbol of our past,
and Christmas, not your future."

I get up and go to her. "I understand what you're saying,
Franco. Please don't say it again." Franco puts her mother's
wedding band in my hand. I put it on my finger.

"You asked me about death, and I said I hoped it wasn't a
big nothing. What I believe is that some part of me, my spirit
or my consciousness, goes on. I don't think I'll be gone from
you entirely, and if you need to feel me near you, I will be able
to comfort you in some way, in a spiritual way. But I don't want
you to need me too much. I want you to get on with your life."

"You're saying it again," I say.

"Will you try to do that?" she asks.

"I will," I answer.

"You'll be surprised, Thad, you're going to be happy. Truly
happy."

"Without you?"

"Once you decide to be," Franco says, and she scoots down
under the covers, pulling me along with her.

I can feel the length of Franco against me, her legs touching
mine, her hips, her stomach, her breasts, her arms around me,
and I think, her spirit will never be the comfort her body is.

Friday, December 27
Woodbine to San Francisco

Dressed for my journey, I give the rooms upstairs one last look before going down. Cleo is with me, following me from Franco's bedroom to the bathroom, where she gets waylaid by a bird at the feeder, and surprises me a moment later by leaping up on the bed in the guest room. I reach out my hand to pet her. Someday I will be her person. Brushing tears from my cheeks, I go back to the bathroom to collect myself. I want to be composed for Franco. I want her to remember me strong. I take the cap off her cologne bottle and dab some on me, then head downstairs with my suitcase.

I can smell bacon cooking and can hear conversation coming from the kitchen. Franco is talking to someone on the phone. I pass through the kitchen and into Franco's office. A walnut pencil box is on her desk. I open it, and inside there are at least four dozen microscope slides. Beside the pencil box on Franco's desk is a black fountain pen. I lift it to my lips. It smells like Franco. I glance up at the photos on the wall above the desk, then step back and scan the room. A small print of Woodbine College is propped up against books on one of the bookshelves. When I turn to leave the room, I see Franco in the open doorway, looking in at me. She has that intensely intimate expression on her face.

"Imagine you loving me," she says. "That was Nell on the phone. She wanted to speak with you before you left, but didn't want to interrupt our good-bye so she settled for talking to me."

"Are you saying I don't have to call her back?"

"You didn't want to, did you?"

"I'll write to her," I say.

"Are you hungry?"

"Yes, I am," I say, and Franco turns to go put breakfast on the table. I make a sound, and she turns back around to look at me.

"I don't know what that was," I say. Was it my stomach crying at the prospect of some food, or my heart crying at the prospect of my leaving?

We sit at the kitchen table to eat our breakfast. I haven't eaten since yesterday's breakfast, and my stomach is confused. I feel a wave of nausea with my first bite and then I am ravenous. Franco's hand trembles and interrupts her eating, but rather than trying to hide this from me, we watch it together. When her hand recovers I glance up at Franco. I want to say something but cannot.

After breakfast we go into the living room. Franco sits on the couch, and I go to the window and look out. It seems like a lifetime ago, not a week ago, that I arrived here.

"You'll write to me?" I say.

"Yes, of course, I will," she answers.

"And if you wake up in the middle of the night from a nightmare, will you call me?"

"I will," Franco answers.

"And other times?"

"Yes."

I step over to the couch and sit down beside Franco. We are like two lovers in a railroad station, waiting for the train that will take one of us away. We cannot look at one another. We look down at our hands and at the floor.

"It's time for me to go," I say.

Franco gets up with me, and we walk to the front door. I put on my coat.

"I'm going to miss you, Thad."

I try to smile. It feels contorted.

"It was easier to be me," she says, and when she adds, "always," I shake my head. "Yes, it was, Thad. I don't know how you risked so much. With your heart, I know, but I don't know how."

"I love you," I say, and I put my arms around Franco.

"It goes deeper than that."

"Nothing goes deeper than that," I say, and we kiss, and the glorious physical world returns to us.

"I wanted to feel, Franco, and I have. I have felt all the things I ever longed to feel." I reach for the handle on my suitcase.

"I love you, Thad."

"Good-bye, Franco."

When I turn and open the door, her hand touches the back of my head. I don't turn around, but on the front walk I stop to look back at the house and see Franco's face framed in the windowpane. I will never have to do anything as hard as this, I tell myself, as I turn away from her and take my next step.

On the drive to the airport I reassure myself that I can always come back. I can come back in two days, in two weeks, or in two months. I won't, but allowing myself to think that makes it possible for me to drive on.

I wear my sunglasses on the plane ride home. I look at no one and I speak to no one.

In San Francisco, the taxi driver tries to make conversation with me. I ignore him and think about Edna. She will be glad to see me, I reckon, and for her, life will resume as though there had been no interruption.

As soon as Edna hears my key in the lock, she starts to bark. When I open the door she is there, licking the air and wagging her tail furiously.

The telephone rings shortly after I arrive home. When it stops

I take it off the hook. I am in no shape to speak to anyone, and it would not be Franco. Franco would not call today. She told me too many times that she wanted me to get on with my life.

Martha has left a note on the kitchen table.

"Welcome home," it says. "Edna and I are glad you're back, and I, at least, don't expect the feeling to be mutual. She was sweet company for me, Thad. I will speak with you soon, and in the meantime I am thinking of you, Martha."

I turn after reading Martha's note and look out the kitchen window at my garden below. The pink azalea bush is in bloom. It's a shock after all that white snow.

No one is around to see or hear me. I cry out to Franco, and the horrible sound I make upsets Edna. She paws at the back of my legs until I sink to the kitchen floor and she can climb onto my lap. We sit there for some time before we go out for a walk to the Broadway and Baker steps where we went when I got Franco's letter.

The bay is choppy today; there is only an oil freighter on it, no sailboats. I look around me at all the familiar landmarks which seem strange and impersonal today.

"Thad?" someone hollers, and I turn quickly, expecting Franco, creating in that instant a story of how she followed me home.

"I've been calling and calling!" Martha says, out of breath.

"What are you doing here?" I ask.

"The operator said something was wrong with your phone."

"I took it off the hook."

"I got worried. Are you O.K.? When did you get back?"

"An hour ago."

"How was it?"

I shake my head. I don't want to talk to Martha or to anyone. I want to be alone, left alone.

Martha moves toward me, hesitates, then sits down beside me on the step.

"I don't think I can talk about it," I say.

"Let's walk then," she says.

If I can't sit by myself I might as well walk, I think.

Martha and Edna and I start down Broadway toward the Presidio and continue into the park. The path we take is shaded and smells of the eucalyptus trees which line it.

"I'm torn apart," I say, thinking after I've said this that I shouldn't have said anything. Martha puts a hand on my shoulder. "You've got to watch what you ask for," I say, pulling away from her gently. "I used to think if Franco would open up to me my world would be perfect. And far from being perfect, it is torn apart. I don't know how I'm going to get along without her."

"I was afraid you were going to say you and she didn't get along."

"I don't want to be here, Martha. I want to be with her."

"Why aren't you?"

"She wants to do this alone."

"It might be harder for her if you were there."

"And she wants me to get on with my life."

"And that's hard for you to understand?"

"What life?" I say, and I stop walking and cover my face with my hands. I don't want to cry in front of Martha. I don't want to be exposed like this. I want to run away and be by myself.

Martha gives me a moment, and then she says, "I wish there was something I could say to help you. I love you, Thad. I care that you're in such pain."

I'm surprised to hear Martha say she loves me and I wish she hadn't. She notices it has made me uneasy and she says, "Don't we all, Thad? Franco's not unique in that, you know."

This doesn't make me feel any better, Martha speaking of Franco in this way.

"I'll walk you back," Martha says, perhaps sensing my displeasure, "and if you want me to leave you alone, I will."

Thank God, I think.

We walk in silence and when we get to my place I invite Martha in for a sherry. I feel I must because she took care of Edna and because she is being kind.

Martha and I settle in the living room, at enough of a distance to make it possible for me to relax. I have the opposite problem with Martha that I once had with Franco. Martha likes to be so close that often I feel crowded by her.

"Is the ring new?" she asks after a moment.

"It was her mother's," I answer. Martha maybe doesn't know what to make of this. She doesn't say anything. "Franco wants me to go back at the end," I say, "and be with her when she dies."

Again, Martha says nothing; this time she turns her face away from my view.

"She thinks that will be soon," I say, and I hear Martha say she is sorry. When she turns her face back to me, I see tears on her cheeks.

She wipes them away and asks, "How do you bear it?"

"The ache has been such constant company it feels like a friend."

"I hope not," she says.

"What about you?" I ask. "What's happening with you and Ned?"

"It's over for us. I know I hinted that if he got sick of her I'd take him back, but after this week I realize I wouldn't. I've been less lonely without Ned than I was with him. I want more than what we had."

"Maybe it's not possible to get everything you want."

"I don't expect to get it all, but it was no good feeling like I was there for him, that I belonged to him. Do women do that to one another?"

"I'm no expert," I say, to avoid getting into the subject.

"Listen, Thad, I think I'm going to stay. You seem better with me."

I don't want Martha to stay. I want to be alone with my thoughts and feelings. If Martha stays I'll have to engage in conversation. I'll have to listen to her and pretend interest. I don't have the strength or the desire to do that.

"You're not saying anything," she says.

"I'd rather be alone, Martha."

"I don't think it's a good idea. I'm going to fix you dinner and sleep on your couch. I wouldn't sleep a wink tonight, worrying about you here alone your first night, and to tell you the truth, I'm not crazy about going back to my empty loft. You can do whatever you want. Go for a walk, take a bath, go to bed."

Of course I *should* be able to do whatever I want, but if you stay I won't be free to.

"If I stick around," Martha continues, "then I can be your friend instead of that ache."

I can almost hear Franco saying, Let *her stay*, Thad. *It will be good for you*.

"I'll scrounge up some grub," Martha says, and against my will I am nodding my head.

"I'm going to take Edna over to Alta Plaza," I say, getting up from my seat.

"You know, Thad," Martha says, stopping Edna and me before we can get out the door, "you're a great-looking woman. I see the way people look at you."

"Please, Martha."

"If I had your eyes and your figure, I'd set the world on fire."

"I'm not interested in setting the world on fire," I say.

"I know," she says.

I force a smile and say, "And if you were really me, you wouldn't either."

"I know," she says again, and Edna and I leave.

On the sidewalk out front I have the feeling I made a narrow escape. God Almighty, what have I got myself into tonight?

The sun is starting to set, and the light is extraordinary. Buildings have a pinkish cast, and the trees and grass have a yellow glow. I'm glad, at least, to be going to the park where I can sit on the bench overlooking the bay and think whatever comes into my mind.

The elegant woman with the wolfhound is at the park.

"You're back," she says when she sees me.

I suppose I appear taken aback by her remark because she explains that when she saw someone else with Edna she asked about me. We introduce ourselves. Her name is Elizabeth.

I stay at the park as long as I think I can get away with it, knowing if I stay too long Martha will come out looking for me and spoil any chance I may have for a quiet walk home.

What are you up to now? I wonder about Franco. Have you gone to bed? Do you miss me? Does it seem to you as though I was never there? I picture our Christmas tree and Franco going through her photo album while I decorate it, and leaving it to go to Nell's, and returning home to make love. And these images do not make me feel lonesome. Bolstered by them, I am ready to face Martha.

To my great astonishment, Martha behaves nothing like I expect her to. Far from scrounging up a dinner, Martha has grilled a swordfish and steamed carrots to go with it. She has set a beautiful table in the kitchen with a linen cloth I haven't seen in months, and she has put music on. And all of this without any nuance of romance. Our conversation over dinner is initiated by me; Martha doesn't ask me a single question nor volunteer anything about herself. After dinner I unpack my suitcase, take a shower, and when I return to my bedroom I see my bed has been turned down. I go to the living room and find Martha sitting on the couch, reading a book.

"You won't sleep there, I hope. You'll sleep in the guest room?"

She nods her head, and I stand gazing at her, puzzled by her quiet countenance. "Do you have everything you need?" she asks me.

"Yes, I do, Martha. Thank you for dinner."

"You're welcome, Thad."

"What kind of mother did you have?" I ask her.

"Standard variety," she says.

"Did she pull down your bed at night and tuck you in?"

Martha gives a nod.

"I'm grateful," I say.

"Good-night," she says. "If you need me—"

"I don't think I will," I say.

"I don't mind being waked up at any hour, but you'll have to give me a good shake because I sleep so soundly."

I bet she does, I think, finding my vision of her sprawled out in bed, sound asleep, both amusing and comforting.

"Good-night," I say.

Saturday, December 28
San Francisco

I wake up in my bed, knowing where I am. I would rather be confused than feel this certainty that I will not see Franco's face this morning, nor all day long, nor the next day, nor the day that follows that.

Edna's whine gets me out of bed to go feed her. Martha is in the kitchen, sitting at the table, dressed. She doesn't stick around after breakfast. She has things to do.

I don't get dressed when Martha leaves. I spend the day going from room to room, pacing, standing, unwilling to sit, to settle in. Edna takes on my restless mood and follows me everywhere I go until, finally, I put her out in the backyard. I've had it, I think. I'm tired of making the effort to get on and get along.

Sunday, December 29
San Francisco

I have nothing worth saying.

Monday, December 30
San Francisco

I don't want to resume life here.

Tuesday, December 31
New Year's Eve

I get up to feed Edna and go back to bed. I don't get up again for hours, and then only to have a bowl of cereal. My one concern is what I will do about Edna. I try to think of someone I could give her to.

The telephone rings and wakes me around 6:00 P.M. It's Carol. She wants to see me. I don't want to see her, so I say next week. She says she *must* see me tonight. She sounds in trouble. I say O.K. and get up. I don't make my bed but I do get dressed.

Carol doesn't arrive until 10:00 P.M. She spent Christmas in St. Thomas with a new friend and is suntanned. I resent her telling me she had to see me, as though she were in trouble, then waltzing in here with a suntan and good news on her way to a New Year's Eve party.

After a drink, Carol tells me she is still in love with me and doesn't know how to get over it. I listen to her and tell her I haven't got an answer for her, that I'm in the same boat. She wants to know who I'm in love with, and I won't tell her. She wants to kiss me when she leaves. I won't let her, and she leaves upset. I feel badly for denying her such a little thing.

The phone rings a short while later. I don't answer it because I think it might be Carol. The ringing stops and a moment later it starts up again. This time I pick it up. It's Franco.

"I called to tell you I love you," Franco says, sounding cheerful. I don't respond. I don't know why I can't.

"Thad?"

"Yes, I'm here," I answer.

"You sound strange."

"I am strange," I say.

"What have you been doing?"

"Nothing."

"Have you tried to do anything?" Franco asks.

"No."

"Why not?"

"I'm tired of trying."

"You're giving up, is that it?"

"That's it, Franco."

"Then don't drag it out, Thad. Take some pills and get it over with."

I'm stunned. How could she say this to me? I don't say anything and neither does she for what seems like a long while.

Then she says, "Good-bye, Thad."

"No! Don't!" I shout into the phone. "Don't hang up."

"Why not? You're giving up."

"Please."

"Thad, this is going to be hard for you to hear, but it's got to be said. Either you get on with your life and continue to be my friend, or you give up. If you've decided to give up, there's no reason for us to continue to be friends."

"I don't know how to go on," I say.

"That's not true. You do know how."

"I can't think of a reason to, Franco."

"Because you assume nothing good is ahead for you. You don't know that. You sure don't know that."

"I'm not inspired. I'm tired."

"Distract yourself. Do something, anything. Get out. You sure as hell aren't going to be inspired by wallowing in your pain."

"I'm not wallowing."

"Sure you are."

"Maybe I need to."

"Thad, think of a place, a favorite place, a meadow or a lakeside or a hilltop. And not a place where you and I have been." It is quiet for a while and then Franco asks, "Are you doing that?"

"No."

"Do it! Right now while I hang on."

"O.K."

Again it is quiet, and then she asks, "Have you got it?"

"Yes."

"Have you got it pictured in detail?"

"Yes," I answer.

"Can you see yourself there? Feel the earth under you and the sun on you and smell the air?"

"Yes, Franco."

"Good. Now, I'm going to say good-night and hang up. I want you to call me tomorrow. And in the meantime, when you feel like you want to give up, go to that place. Close your eyes and imagine yourself there, and when you are there, ask yourself how to go on."

"I miss you, Franco."

"And call me tomorrow," she says.

"I will," I answer.

Franco says good-night, and I wait for the click of her receiver. I look at the clock. It is almost midnight, the end of a year.

Wednesday, January 1
San Francisco

All morning I put off calling Franco because I'll have nothing to look forward to after I have. At one o'clock I can't wait any longer.

"Hello," Franco says, in her private voice, sounding softer and deeper than she would otherwise sound.

"Did you know it would be me?" I ask.

"Yes."

"I'm having trouble, Franco."

"I can hear it in your voice."

"I want to come back."

"It will get easier for you. How are you doing with your place?"

"Not great. How are you doing? And if you say you're doing great—"

"I miss you, Thad."

"Then I'm returning."

"No, not yet."

"I never imagined anything this hard. I thought I'd had some hard times but nothing like this."

"When you get over the idea that you can't make it without

me, you'll be fine."

"Franco, why do you always take such a hard line?"

"You force me to."

"How do I force you to?"

"If you were braver, I could ease up."

"I love you, Franco. I'd give anything to be able to touch you right now."

"Yes, I know how you feel."

"How are you feeling?"

"Tired. Let's talk about you. What are you doing today?"

"No plans."

"You should have some. Why don't you go over to the Marine Mammal Center?"

"I suppose I could."

"Do it. And tomorrow?"

"Tomorrow I return all those damn bluebooks I graded. What about you?"

"Tomorrow Nell's coming over to break in someone who's going to be cleaning the house."

"I'm jealous."

"You're a lost cause, Thad."

"That's what I've been trying to tell you."

"The most beautiful lost cause I ever knew. Be brave and write to me."

"Don't hang up yet."

"What are you holding on to, Thad?"

"You."

"Yes, I can sure feel it."

"I'm sorry, Franco. I would like to be wiser and braver."

"I don't want you to be sorry. You know that I'm not your all and everything and that you can be happy without me. That's why you won't let yourself. It wouldn't be a betrayal if you were happy, Thad."

"I'm *not* sure I can be happy without you, Franco."

"Of course you're not sure, but give yourself a chance. There's more to you than the you and me part. I don't believe that your happiness is limited to that . . .Thad?"

"I'm thinking about what you said."

"Be brave and write to me."

"I will," I answer.

"I love you."

"I love you, Franco."

When I hang up the phone I put on my jacket, and Edna and I go over to the Marin Headlands.

Saturday, January 4
San Francisco

My first letter from Franco arrives.

Dear Thad,

I *took down our* Christmas tree today. I *lifted off each ornament and untangled the string of lights with special care, thinking about us as* I *did.* I *even looked around once or twice, imagining you were here. And when she was naked again, a bit more yellow than the day we picked her out of the crowd,* I *took a picture of her. But there's really no way of holding on, is there? Just the same* I'm *getting it developed to give to you.*

Since then I've *clipped the branches off our tree and gathered them together in a basket. They will make the room smell nice for a week or two.*

It *was a fine Christmas, Thad. My very best!*

I *love you,*
Franco

Monday, January 13
Nine days later

Dear Thad,

The snow is gone. Three warm days in a row did it, but it's supposed to get cold and snow again tonight. Nell found me someone to shovel the walk when it does. I tried to do it, but I can't do it good enough to suit me.

Irene and her kids left for Ohio Thursday. They came over here on their way out of town, and Irene and I chatted for a few minutes. She wanted your address. You made quite a hit with her. She told me if Ohio doesn't work out, she's going to move to California.

Birds are at the feeder early every morning and just before dusk. I have had to fill it twice already. Good thing we moved it under the window. Cleo now sits on the bathroom sill, watching and making those horrible throat sounds. I filled the tub one morning last week, then left the bathroom to do something. When I came back in I startled Cleo, and she fell off the sill and into the tub. I wish you had been here to see her dog paddle.

I'm writing a paper on my protein for Discover magazine. Have gotten a lot of mileage out of that. If I finish it in time it will be in the April issue. I know that sounds like a long ways off, but I have to turn it in in two weeks. I am feeling like a student under the gun.

I can't tell you how glad I am that you have joined the living! And that you are writing instead of calling. It's not that I don't miss the sound of your voice. I do. But I can hold your letters and read them over and over and refer to them at any time of day or night. Keep it up. And don't make something out of the fact that I write half as often. It is harder for me. I DO NOT LOVE YOU LESS.

I love you,
Franco

P.S. Why don't you send me something you've made in pottery class!

Friday, January 31
Two weeks later

Ten days pass and I do not hear from Franco. My imagina-
tion runs wild with reasons why, and I call her. Four days later
I get this letter from her:

Dear Thad,

I'm sorry that I haven't written and that I couldn't talk
longer on the phone. Now you know the reason is this lousy
cold. I'm sure one of the DePaul kids gave it to me.

Don't read any more of that stuff on ALS. It just makes
you worry about gruesome things you don't need to think
about. My shortness of breath when you were here, and on
the phone, does not mean I have that kind of ALS or that
I've graduated to the advanced stages. I'm sure this trouble
I have now and again is anxiety and nothing more. I'm not
going to choke to death in the middle of the night. I know
that's what you're afraid of and don't say. Relax.

Your teaching schedule sounds ideal. You ought to put those
four-day weekends to good use. Go away to Yosemite or Men-
docino. I don't miss teaching at all. Everyone said I wouldn't
be any good not having something I had to do, and they were

wrong. I like this. I'm reading a lot. Nell brings me things, and I have journals that are three years old that I haven't looked at. I don't care that the stuff isn't current. That's one good thing about this predicament of mine. I don't have to have a "purpose" to everything I do. I don't have to be on top of things. And almost no one can make me feel guilty for not doing something they want me to do. I guess you know why I had to say almost.

I am reading a book I want you to try to locate. If you can't, I will send you my copy when I finish with it. It is Stewart Edward White's The Unobstructed Universe. And please send me some of your pottery. I forgot to remind you of that on the phone.

Thad, that's all I can do for you for now.

I love you,
Franco

Friday, February 7
A week later

Dear Thad,

I love the porcelain egg! I got it two days ago, and it hasn't been out of my sight except at night when it is under my pillow, on the off chance that the Good Fairy would exchange it for a new nervous system.

I'm over my cold and enjoying life as much as anyone could under the circumstances. I can hear you: What are your circumstances? I am dragging around, not much worse off than I was a month ago.

My happiest moments are reading your letters. I'm entertained by them and reassured, but most of all it feels as though you are sitting on the edge of the bed with me. I read them over and over for that.

Yes, I do wish sometimes that you were here. Above all, I miss your warmth. Sometimes when I concentrate very hard, I almost feel you next to me.

I love you,
Franco

Monday, February 17
Ten days later

Dear Thad,

I got anxious the other night and called you, but you weren't home. Good thing, because it would have alarmed you unnecessarily. By morning I felt better, and today I am doing very well.

Nell has come by every day since my cold. Today I sent her home. At last I have my privacy back. No one but Cleo to answer to.

Writing this is slow going, but I couldn't hold on to a pen if my life depended upon it a day ago. My legs are weaker, too, one worse than the other, but I get around at a snail's pace.

Yes, I did get the paper done in time—Nell typed it for me, and no, I didn't get Irene's address in Ohio. Nell has it and will send it to you.

I'm learning quite a lot from Betty White, which you will understand when you read Stewart's book. I'm not surprised you can't find it, even in San Francisco. Its copyright is 1940, I think. I will send it to you when I finish.

Yes, do send me any books you think might be enjoyable and useful. Nell brings over all sorts of things: poems by once-

upon-a-time students of hers—one of yours turned up—nice,
too; old record albums, and photographs of people I don't know.
She's nuts, of course, and it interests me that she doesn't seem
to care that I might think she is.

I'm going out now to bring wood in for the fireplaces. Nell
was going to get the kid who shovels the walk to do it, but
it will make my day if I can do it myself. I have been inactive
for weeks. I need to test myself, give myself a reason to hold
on, see if there is any reason to, and breathe in some fresh air.

I love you,
Franco

Thursday, February 27
Two months since I last saw Franco

Dear Thad,

Thank you for that letter. I would like to know what caused the change, but if you'd rather not say, that would be O.K. I'm grateful for it, and I can't begin to tell you how relieved. My concern for Cleo is nothing compared to my concern for you. You have reassured me and made my life easier. Friends and family who are left behind, especially those who know they will be left behind, have the hardest part in the play. I know you worry about doing your part well. You also have your terrible predicament to cope with. I don't expect your performance to be flawless. All that just to say thank you, it's more than I expected, and I won't be distraught if it can't be maintained at all times.

I sent you the book yesterday. Nell did, actually. Afterward she picked up some crutches for me to get around on. They are the aluminum kind that are lightweight and ugly. I hate them, Thad. I won't use them.

I hope you'll find what Betty White says as credible as I do. But, having said that, if you don't please say so. I'd hate for you to agree just for the sake—who am I thinking of? Not *us, certainly!*

I don't mention my family in letters because my conversations with them and their letters to me are aggravating. "Why can't I come see you?" "Why are you avoiding us?" "Don't you care how we feel?" Maybe I'm nuts not to want people doting on me; it sure is hard for everyone to understand.

Nell and I had a fight last night. I got angry with her because she tried to help me eat my dinner. She said it was obvious I needed help. I said I didn't and accused her of being impatient because I was taking too long. She said I was the hardest person in the world to do something for. I said she was angry because I wasn't more grateful. She said she didn't need my gratitude, but I sure as hell needed her, so I better close my trap before it was too late. I did. There was a ring of truth in what she said.

I felt like a wretch afterward. And again this morning. Thank God for your letter. I couldn't be the worst person in the world if you thought so much of me.

I sign I love you to my letters because I never said it enough. Aren't you funny to ask about that.

I will call you on your birthday.

I love you,
Franco

Franco's letter refers to one I wrote, confessing that although I had returned to my life, I had been carrying her around with me everywhere I went, distracted by my painful longing for her, and that I'd done enough of that. I told Franco I left her at home one day and discovered I could manage on my own.

The event which precipitated this happened weeks before my letter to Franco. A colleague at school took me aside and said that since I'd returned from the break I hadn't looked well. I told her why, and she told me her sister's only child was in Shriner's hospital, dying. That night she took me to a group for family members in crisis. It was pointed out to me that I could cling to Franco, or I could let her go, and I should understand that choosing to do the first was not an act of love but a struggle for possession which was futile and destructive. I left the session feeling terrible, defensive about my *unique* situation, and angry with the colleague who had taken me. I realized that what I'd been told was true. Gradually I opened myself up to it and began to let go of Franco.

Saturday, March 8
Nine days later

Dear Thad,

I'm so glad I called you. The sound of your voice picked me up from a low place. I didn't want to tell you I'm losing ground. Not on your birthday. But I think you guessed I am.

Nell is here now four days a week. No nights unless I have a really bad day. She and I talk about my dying. Maybe that is why I haven't written about it. If you feel jealous over this, I can only say that that is her role in this, and although you may wish it was yours, it isn't because I didn't want it to be.

I don't feel anxious about getting worse, but I do feel sad sometimes. Yesterday I read the poems you sent, took a bath, and cried. I hadn't cried since you were here. I didn't enjoy it, but I did feel better afterward. I try to feel sure of the things Betty White promises, and at times I do. But I don't do my part perfectly, either. I have moments when I am strong, and that's all—moments. When I am weak I am a difficult case for Nell.

It snowed again today. Enough is enough!

Please send me photographs of the flowers in your backyard. And of you. You are my joy.

I *love you,*
Franco

Tuesday, March 18
Ten days later

Dear Thad,

I don't think I have been vague about what's happening and how I feel about it. It's not true that I have always gotten my way with you, and this here is proof of that:

I'm typing this letter because I can't write clearly. The tremors and weakness are worse. No one likes to see the tremors, so any guests I have don't hang around. I consider that a blessing. I can't walk without help, so when I'm alone or just Nell is here I scoot along on my fanny. I don't mind Nell seeing me behave like a toddler, but when someone else is around I act like an adult and stay put. You can imagine I feel very trapped when people are visiting. I cope with all my limitations and discomforts better when I am alone. I would like to live thirty more years, at least. I didn't expect my life to be so short. I distract myself with pleasant thoughts, with books, and with TV when I am feeling bad. And I don't dwell on things that are bound to make me feel sad. With one exception: I think of you, and thoughts of you make me happy and sad.

So there you have it, answers to all your boring questions.

I *love you,*
Franco

P.S. I *asked* Nell *to read this to make certain I was direct
and clear. She says I sound angry and that if I'm not I should
rewrite it in a more pleasant tone. I'm not angry, Thad. The
sharp edge is only there because I am uncomfortable today.*

Thursday, March 27
Three months since I saw Franco

Dear Thad,

The college chaplain was just by to see me, and I was annoyed by his visit. He kept reassuring me that I would be with my Father in heaven. And that God gave His only begotten Son so that I might have life everlasting. Finally I said that I'd feel more reassured if I thought I'd be with my Mother in heaven. He looked at me so perplexed. Nell showed him out and then apologized for showing him in in the first place.

"Did you hear what he said?" I asked her.

"If we can put a man on the moon, why not all of them," she answered.

"Boy, did he annoy me," I snarled.

"Like a sandwich in a horse's tail," she said, and did we ever laugh.

At long last, winter may be behind us. I suppose it's strange of me to rush into the future, but instead of thinking of my demise, I look forward to everything coming alive soon. There's a purple hyacinth on the table by the couch, narcissus in the bedroom, and cattails on the dining room table. I look out on grass which is more brown than green, but it won't be long until it is growing. And the trees have their first small buds.

Tomorrow is supposed to be even warmer than today, and Nell and I are going to have a picnic. Just in the backyard, but I can't tell you how I'm looking forward to that.

I asked you to send me pictures of your yard and of you, and you sent me two of your yard. I want a recent photograph of you. I miss you and I'm tired of looking at old photographs of you.

You mentioned my searching you out and coming to see you in the infirmary years ago. What I remember most about that day is that I wanted to tell you I was in love with you. I wanted to say that to you countless times and didn't because I wanted first to be sure you felt the same. I don't know how many weeks passed before you crawled into bed with me. It was probably fewer than it seemed. I know the next day I disappointed you by being standoffish, and I've regretted that a hundred times. I was a coward, Thad. You were brave and wonderful, coming to my bed, and I was afraid because I'd lost the upper hand. My coolness was an attempt to gain it back. What a foolish thing to want.

When I met you I was captivated by your physical beauty. I had my first real glimpse inside you when we went home for your grandmother's funeral, and you told me the truth about your parents. For all my bravado, I haven't nearly the courage you have. I have known for a very long time that you could and would outdistance me.

I love you,
Franco

Wednesday, April 9
Two weeks later

Dear Thad,

Thanks for the picture. You look wonderful, and so does
Edna. I have you in a frame beside my bed along with your
egg which is in an old nest Nell found in the backyard last
week.

Speaking of pictures, I just got my April issue of Discover,
and there isn't a picture of me with the article. They came
to the house with cameras—two photographers. Don't ask me
why. Maybe someone warned them about me and neither
would come alone. And they took one look at me, decided
I wasn't the picture of health, and asked me if I had a favorite
picture I would like to have accompany my article. I said I
didn't want a picture that didn't look like me, so they took
a picture of me, but that was only for show. I guess I shouldn't
be surprised that it was omitted on the grounds that I might
remind folks of their mortality.

Now my real news: Three days ago my family descended
upon Nell and me. Louise and John from Chicago, Ellen from
Ohio, Patrick and Diane all the way from San Diego, and
Peg. They cooked up this trip among themselves and elected

Ellen to call me from the college inn to tell me they were here. Nell took it better than I did.

"No one listened to a damn thing I said!" I hollered, after hanging up the phone with Ellen.

"For a pragmatist, your expectations have a touch of the unreal," is what Nell said.

I was scared, Thad. About them seeing me looking like I do. And Nell, a stranger to vanity, didn't understand what I was concerned about. She didn't know what the hell to do for me since she didn't understand my complaint. We had only an hour to get me spruced up and on the couch. We did our best. I was no Miss America.

The gang arrived just after noon and stayed for dinner. Nell made spaghetti. Nell, I'm certain, has a reserved seat at the right hand of God.

They all walked in looking tense and sad. Except Peg, who looked better than I've seen her look in years. And it was plenty awkward at first. You know, no one saying anything, then all at once everyone saying something polite and meaningless. Finally I said, "All right you guys, let's drop the masquerade. This isn't a birthday party."

Louise started to cry, and John, as self-conscious as the day he married her, could only pat Louise's arm to comfort her.

"Come here," I said to her, and Louise came and sat down on the couch with me and we hugged. It was nice, Thad. Your kind of thing. I felt just like you and realized I was doing you.

Then Patrick got up from the chair he was sitting in and got down on the floor by me. Diane followed him, then Ellen and Peg. And after rocking back and forth for a moment or two, John came and huddled with us. I told them what was going on with me, and then they talked quietly about their lives, each of them taking turns. Peg said she was going to A.A. I swear, Thad, it was almost like holidays when we converged at the folks' place. Except Dan and David and you were missing. Nell even reminded me of Mom.

We ate early because I'm not much good after six. And

after supper, Peg and Louise and Diane cleaned up while John and Pat went out to the shed, got out the ladder, took down the storms and put up the screens, and then cleaned out the gutters. Ellen came upstairs with Nell and me.

Once I was settled in bed, Nell left, and Ellen and I talked. And all the while we were talking we could hear the two men outside, calling to one another and joking. For a while there I think we both felt the years had peeled away.

Ellen has lived alone since David died. She told me she has been enjoying her solitude, and she apologized for the day's invasion. I confessed that when they walked in I was furious with them all, but that I was glad now that they had come. Then I told Ellen about Christmas, and she said she would love to see you again. It dawned on both of us at the same moment that she would get her chance soon. She made a face, but then she smiled. We didn't have to say anything.

Before leaving, Ellen said, ''When David died something wonderful happened which I've never told anyone. He came to visit me, Frances. Not as his old self or like a ghost. It was more like he was in the other room. I didn't see him or hear him, but I knew he was there. After that I never felt desolate. I missed David, but not in that excruciating way. And I have never doubted that he lives on.''

I thanked Ellen for telling me all that, and her last words to me were, ''I'll be expecting you.''

One at a time the others came up after Ellen left, to say good-bye. It wasn't perfect. Patrick wanted to be cheerful, but his face was anything but. And Diane and I don't know one another, so it was awkward for her. John kissed me on the cheek, a polite kiss. Louise took my hand and gave it a squeeze, then hugged me. She wanted to say something but couldn't. Peg said she'd see me soon, and I gave her a look like the hell you will. I saw her shrink and I felt like the wicked sister, so I quickly said I'd be calling her. Then I told Peg to get Ellen back up because I had something to tell her.

Ellen came in, sat down on the bed, and waited for me to

tell her what was on my mind. I said I just wanted her face to be the last. She winked, gave me a kiss, and left without a word. Ellen will be glad to see you, Thad, and I feel good about that.

And now I'm too pooped to write any more.

I *love you*,
Franco

Monday, April 28
Nineteen days later

Dear Thad,

I'm sliding past the point of insisting I do things for myself, so Nell is typing this. I say sliding because that is how
it feels, like sliding on Woodbine's frozen pond, out of control
and perhaps heading for disaster, but enjoying the sensation
which is, at times, exhilarating.

Spring is here! Nell went out this morning to pick up some
things and returned with branches of quince and forsythia she
had taken from someone's yard. She insists upon adding that
she got permission to prune her neighbor's bushes. See how
it is when someone does you a favor; they can't help but in-
sert themselves.

I dreamed of you last night. We were in Michigan, and
you were showing me that tree you climbed as a child to peer
out at the world. You climbed up into it, out of sight, and
I waited for you to return to me, but you didn't. I called to
you and you didn't answer, so I climbed up after you and
you flew from the tree like a bird. Your arms were stretched
out, your legs straight back and parted slightly, and your
thighs were very large, like Picasso's Three Women Danc-

ing. You were naked, and the sun was shining on you, making you look golden. At first I was hurt because you flew away from me, but you were so beautiful to watch, my hurt dissolved into something like awe.

Nell says I'm the bird, idealized as you. I told her I wouldn't be in awe of myself, and she just looked at me.

I'm glad you have been talking to Martha. I don't expect you to be silent about me or us, and I never want you to be.

I love you,
Franco

Wednesday, May 14
Written in Nell's hand

Dear Thad,
  I *want to see you. Please come when the semester ends.*

                                        I *love you,*
                                        Franco

Franco's letters were my obsession for nearly six months. Away at school, I wondered if a letter from her had arrived that day. Returning home, the first thing I did was look for one. And finding one, I carried it around with me until the next arrived. This was the last, I reckoned, and I realized that it was another in a series of last things.

After dinner, I called Franco on the phone and spoke to her briefly. She sounded good. Her voice was less forceful but cheerful. She told me she had things to do during the next two weeks, and she didn't want to see me before school ended.

Friday, May 30-Thursday, June 5
Woodbine and San Francisco

I took the same flight east I'd taken at Christmas time, but this time when I arrived it was still light out. Franco's cobblestone house looked just as I'd remembered it the summer I went east to tell Franco I wanted to move back to live with her. The flower beds were full, the trees were thick with leaves, and the shed was covered with red roses.

Franco smiled when I stepped into her bedroom. We hugged, and I could feel how slight she had become. Her eyes were no longer bright; they looked tired.

Nell had left only minutes before I arrived, and she would not return until I called her on Sunday morning, June first. She'd left a casserole in the refrigerator for us, which I warmed up for our dinner. We ate upstairs, and afterward I got into bed with Franco and read to her. We slept soundly.

Saturday would be our last day together. I knew this the way you know when anything is complete, when more is unnecessary and only a delay. We spoke very few words that day, the bare minimum. I went out for a walk by myself before dinner. It was a beautiful night. The sky was glowing, birds were at the feeder, the breeze was warm. When I returned home I carried Franco down to the dining room, where we ate dinner. Afterward we returned upstairs, and I put a record on the player which had been moved to Franco's bedroom. The music was low enough that we could hear the spring peepers above it. Franco took what she said was aspirin before going to bed.

I don't know how I kept from waking Franco and forcing her to stay alive, but at one point I was holding on to her too tightly, and she asked me to ease up. I remember the feel of her fanny against my thighs and abdomen and the touch of her hand which held mine.

In the morning it was Franco's voice that woke me.

"It's time to get up," she said, and I opened my eyes.

Franco was still asleep beside me. She had not spoken. She had died in the night.

I don't know how long I stayed there with her and stroked her. In my memory it seems like a short time, but it could have been as long as an hour. When I got up I went downstairs to feed Cleo, and when the two of us returned to the bedroom it was different. Franco was no longer there. It was as though her body was clothing she had once worn. It belonged to the Franco I loved, but it was not Franco.

I opened the thin notebook at the bedside. There were instructions to me and a list of Franco's personal belongings with someone's name next to each item. Franco's house and all its furnishings were to go to the college to be used as a women's residence for visiting professors. In the back of the notebook there were letters to Franco's brother and sisters, and one to me. I opened mine. It was written in Franco's hand.

> My dearest Thad,
>
> Thank you for your great courage and love.
>
> > I love you,
> > Franco

Along with her note was the photograph of our Christmas tree and the paper star that had been on top.

I made calls to Franco's family and to Nell.

Nell was with me when Franco's body was taken away, and afterward she and I went to dinner at the college inn where Franco's family had stayed on their visit.

The next day Ellen arrived to help me wind things up. She stayed at the house with me for two days. There was little for us to do because Franco and Nell had done nearly everything. We wrote letters both mornings, went for a walk the first afternoon, and a drive the second, and ate out both nights. Ellen told me her father had given Franco her nickname, but because there had been so many incidents when Franco was headstrong, Ellen couldn't remember which one had inspired the name. As Ellen spoke, I was thinking of all the things I didn't know about Franco, things I wish I had asked her or insisted she tell me.

Ellen and I went to the airport together yesterday. Her plane took off first, for Cleveland, and Cleo and I left for San Francisco an hour later. Martha and Edna were waiting for us on the front steps when we arrived home.

Last night Cleo slept with me, but this morning when I woke she was gone. I can guess that Edna came in first thing and scared her off. I search everywhere for Cleo and I am about to give in to my worst suspicions, that Edna has eaten her, when I realize where she is. As I lift Cleo out of my clothes hamper I feel the presence of Franco in the room. I stand perfectly still for several moments, enjoying the sensation, and then it fades and Cleo and I go out to the kitchen.

I put Cleo up on the kitchen counter to eat where Edna can't see her or get at her. But Edna knows Cleo is up there, and that sooner or later she's going to come down off that counter. I suppose I'll spend my summer being referee.

Other titles from Firebrand Books include:

The Big Mama Stories by Shay Youngblood/$8.95

A Burst of Light, Essays by Audre Lorde/$7.95

Diamonds Are A Dyke's Best Friend by Yvonne Zipter/$9.95

Dykes To Watch Out For, Cartoons by Alison Bechdel/$6.95

The Fires Of Bride, A Novel by Ellen Galford/$8.95

A Gathering Of Spirit, A Collection by North American Indian Women edited by Beth Brant (*Degonwadonti*)/$9.95

Getting Home Alive by Aurora Levins Morales and Rosario Morales /$8.95

Good Enough To Eat, A Novel by Lesléa Newman/$8.95

Jonestown & Other Madness, Poetry by Pat Parker/$5.95

The Land Of Look Behind, Prose and Poetry by Michelle Cliff /$6.95

A Letter To Harvey Milk, Short Stories by Lesléa Newman/$8.95

Living As A Lesbian, Poetry by Cheryl Clarke/$6.95

Making It, A Woman's Guide to Sex in the Age of AIDS by Cindy Patton and Janis Kelly/$3.95

Metamorphosis, Reflections on Recovery by Judith McDaniel/$7.95.

Mohawk Trail by Beth Brant (*Degonwadonti*)/$6.95

Moll Cutpurse, A Novel by Ellen Galford/$7.95

More Dykes To Watch Out For, Cartoons by Alison Bechdel/$7.95

The Monarchs Are Flying, A Novel by Marion Foster/$8.95

My Mama's Dead Squirrel, Lesbian Essays on Southern Culture by Mab Segrest/$8.95

Politics Of The Heart, A Lesbian Parenting Anthology edited by Sandra Pollack and Jeanne Vaughn/$11.95

Presenting . . . Sister NoBlues by Hattie Gossett/$8.95

A Restricted Country by Joan Nestle/$8.95

Sanctuary, A Journey by Judith McDaniel/$7.95

Shoulders, A Novel by Georgia Cotrell/$8.95

The Sun Is Not Merciful, Short Stories by Anna Lee Walters/$7.95

Tender Warriors, A Novel by Rachel Guido deVries/$7.95

This Is About Incest by Margaret Randall/$7.95

The Threshing Floor, Short Stories by Barbara Burford/$7.95

Trash, Stories by Dorothy Allison/$8.95

The Women Who Hate Me, Poetry by Dorothy Allison/$5.95

Words To The Wise, A Writer's Guide to Feminist and Lesbian Periodicals & Publishers by Andrea Fleck Clardy/$3.95

Yours In Struggle, Three Feminist Perspectives on Anti-Semitism and Racism by Elly Bulkin, Minnie Bruce Pratt, and Barbara Smith/$8.95

You can buy Firebrand titles at your bookstore, or order them directly from the publisher (141 The Commons, Ithaca, New York 14850, 607-272-0000).

Please include $1.75 shipping for the first book and $.50 for each additional book.

A free catalog is available on request.